"Remem_____ **ou**
brough_____ **?"**
Sarah ___

Before_____ con-
fided in_____ hat
with st_____ ne-
thing so good in you, so caring, so decent—"

"Don't paint me a saint, Sarah," he insisted.

"Can I paint you a good friend?" She turned suddenly, smiling. A small glob of blue paint flew off her brush and landed on the tip of his nose.

"Oh, dear," she said, unable to quiet her laughter. "I'm so sorry."

"Did you just paint my nose?" he asked, pretending outrage.

"I'm afraid I did." One giggle escaped, then another, and finally Sarah was caught in a full-blown fit of mirth.

"Lady, when you asked if you could paint me a friend, I didn't think you meant it literally!"

"Blue happens to be your color."

"It is, is it?" Jake touched his nose and his finger came away blue. "I wonder what your color is." And with one swipe he painted a blue streak on her nose. "Now we match."

"Not quite." Sarah bent over the can and came back with blue fingers. He knew what was coming but didn't try to dodge—in fact, he bent down so she could reach him. "Let's see how you look with blue nose *and* cheeks!"

Sarah was standing on tiptoe and he had leaned down. Suddenly the laughter stilled, and awareness sparkled in her eyes. Jake didn't take time to think. He acted on instinct. Sarah's mouth was warm under his. He could taste the heart shape, just as he'd imagined. And it was wonderful. . . .

WHAT ARE *LOVESWEPT* ROMANCES?

They are stories of true romance and touching emotion. We believe those two very important ingredients are constants in our highly sensual and very believable stories in the *LOVESWEPT* line. Our goal is to give you, the reader, stories of consistently high quality that may sometimes make you laugh, sometimes make you cry, but are always fresh and creative and contain many delightful surprises within their pages.

Most romance fans read an enormous number of books. Those they truly love, they keep. Others may be traded with friends and soon forgotten. We hope that each *LOVESWEPT* romance will be a treasure—a "keeper." We will always try to publish

LOVE STORIES YOU'LL NEVER FORGET
BY AUTHORS YOU'LL ALWAYS REMEMBER

The Editors

Loveswept® 538

Peggy Webb
Touched by Angels

BANTAM BOOKS
NEW YORK · TORONTO · LONDON · SYDNEY · AUCKLAND

TOUCHED BY ANGELS

A Bantam Book / April 1992

If you would be interested in receiving protective vinyl
covers for your Loveswept books, please write to this address
for information:

Loveswept
Bantam Books
P.O. Box 985
Hicksville, NY 11802

ISBN 0-553-44199-X

Published simultaneously in the United States and Canada

PRINTED IN THE UNITED STATES OF AMERICA

OPM   0 9 8 7 6 5 4 3 2 1

In memory of Cooper,
who touched all our lives
and gave us a glimpse of angels.

One

The child came out of nowhere.

One minute Jake Townsend was racing down the highway, taking the curves too fast, tempting fate to spare him one more time, and the next minute he was swerving toward the ditch. Dirt and gravel spewed up, hitting his helmet like sudden summer hail. His motorcycle tilted at a crazy angle.

He swore loudly, wrestling with his machine in a life-and-death struggle. The motorcycle came to a bone-jarring stop in the ditch.

Jake jumped free and ran toward the child. She was standing in the middle of the road, sucking her thumb and observing him with enormous eyes. Blue eyes. Bonnie's eyes. Jake froze. The blue eyes regarded him, unblinking. His heart started beating so hard, he nearly lost his breath.

"Bonnie?" he whispered, knowing she wouldn't answer, knowing she could never answer.

The child pulled her thumb from her mouth. It made a soft popping sound.

Jake broke out in a sweat. He passed his hand over

his face. His legs wouldn't move. He was caught in a time warp, trapped in the middle of the dusty road with the blue-eyed child.

Suddenly he heard the car bearing down on them with engine roaring. Jake's paralysis vanished. In one quick motion he grabbed the child and raced to the other side of the road. Dust settled over them as the car whizzed by.

His heart was pumping so hard, he could hear the mad rush of blood in his ears. His legs felt weak.

He looked at the child in his arms. "Oh Lord. I've saved you. Bonnie, I've saved you." He pressed his face to the child's hair. One soft curl clung to his cheek. The morning sun burnished it gold.

Jake's heartbeat slowed and his breathing returned to normal. The child was not Bonnie at all. Bonnie's hair had been dark, almost as dark as his own.

"It's all right, sweetheart," he crooned. "Everything is all right now. You're safe."

The child didn't appear at all frightened. She merely sat in his arms and regarded him with her placid blue eyes.

"What's your name, darling?" Jake asked. But she didn't answer. Maybe she was scared after all, he thought. She looked about four years old. Most four-year-olds told their names when asked. Jake tried again. "Mommy? Where's Mommy?"

"JENNY! JENNY!" The female voice came from behind them.

"I guess that answers my last question." He turned around, still holding on to the unflappable Jenny. The woman racing toward him looked as if she had come straight from combat in a hot and dusty country. Her jeans were grimy, her white blouse was no longer anything to brag about, and her hair straggled from its ponytail. She might have been pretty if she were cleaned up. He couldn't tell. And at the moment he didn't care.

"Is this your child?"

She didn't answer. Instead she plucked the little girl from his arms and cuddled her close. Tears streaked through the dust on her cheeks.

"Jenny," she murmured over and over, "Jenny, my Jenny."

"She's safe," Jake said gently. "Don't worry, she's safe now."

"When I discovered her missing, I was terrified." The mother looked at him with eyes as blue as her child's.

There was something so wise and beautiful about those eyes that Jake wanted to take her into his arms and comfort her. An image of himself as comforter and protector rose up in his mind, and for one glorious golden moment Jake felt human. Warmth and compassion flowed through him, thawing the iceberg that encased his heart. But the moment was fleeting. Caring too much was hell. He'd been there once; he didn't plan to go again.

Jenny and her mother tugged at his heart. *There's danger here*, Jake's mind whispered. He turned away from mother and child—so much temptation, so many memories—and started across the road.

"Wait. I don't even know your name," the woman called after him.

His first instinct was to keep on going. But something made him turn around.

"It's not necessary for you to know my name. We won't be seeing each other again." He would make damned sure of that. He had enough ghosts in his dreams. He didn't want them haunting his waking hours as well.

"I don't blame you for being cross. I'm not a bad

mother." Jenny's mother got fresh tears in her eyes. "It's just that sometimes Jenny gets away. She's . . ." The woman paused, biting her lower lip. ". . . just Jenny."

Jake could never hold firm in the face of a woman's tears. He pulled a handkerchief from his pocket and handed it to her.

"Don't cry. Everything is okay now."

The woman sniffled into the handkerchief while Jenny patted her face. Suddenly the child turned to Jake.

"Mommy sad." There was a faraway quality to Jenny's voice, as if she were bending down from some distant cloud to speak to him.

Jake found himself wondering about mother and child. Who were they? Where had they come from? He had grown up in Florence, Alabama. The house behind them had been vacant for the last five years. It was so old and ramshackle, the local kids used it for a ghost house on Halloween.

"I'm Sarah Love, and this is my daughter, Jenny." The woman extended her hand.

Jake was taken aback, as if she had read his mind. He hesitated for a moment then took her hand. It was soft and smooth, but not at all fragile. There was strength and firmness in Sarah Love's grip. Strength and firmness and a willingness to be friends.

He didn't want to be friends with Sarah Love. He didn't want to know whether she would be merely pretty or simply beautiful in a blue dress that matched her eyes. He didn't want to know whether the rosy glow showing through all the dirt on her face was natural or the result of clever cosmetics.

"I owe you a tremendous debt of thanks," the woman said, smiling through her tears. "You saved Jenny's life."

"You owe me nothing." Jake released her hand. He intended to go quickly, but the child suddenly reached toward him, smiling. Jenny's smile turned his heart upside down. Her dimpled hand waved in the air, and before he knew what he was doing, he had reached for it. It was as light as a dandelion.

"Nice man," Jenny said.

Jake hadn't been nice in six years. Nevertheless he stood by the roadside holding on to Jenny's hand, feeling as if he had just received the Nice Man of the Year award. He fancied that if he looked into the mirror, he might actually see a man who had a heart. He knew that wasn't so, of course. Most people called him cold and many went so far as to call him a heartless bastard. Women, of course, were a different matter. They called him other names, pet names, mainly on the telephone. They called in droves, begging to comfort and soothe him and make him forget. He took their comfort and their soothing, but he never forgot.

And now Jenny was offering comfort. But she was a different matter. She had Bonnie's blue eyes.

"And you're a nice little girl," he said, bending over like a knight in King Arthur's court and pressing a kiss on Jenny's hand. She giggled. Then, feeling a bit foolish, he released her and gave her mother a stern look. "Take care of this child, Sarah Love."

He left quickly before she could reply. He'd had enough of niceness and chivalry for one morning. He climbed onto his motorcycle and revved it to life. He thought he heard Sarah Love's voice over the engine, but he didn't turn off the machine. Nor did he strain his ears to hear. As far as he was concerned, Sarah and Jenny Love were a part of his past, something unexpected that had happened to him on a fine summer morning.

He was careful not to spin out as he drove off in case mother and child were still standing beside the road. He didn't want to send rocks spewing their way. Dust billowed behind him as he raced down the road.

Sarah stood in the dust watching him go. Jenny wiggled in her arms, wanting to get down.

"He didn't even tell me his name," she whispered.

"Nice man," Jenny said.

"Yes, my darling. He was a very nice man." *And he saved your life*, she thought, but she didn't say it aloud. Jenny would not have understood, just as she hadn't understood the danger of wandering into the middle of the road. She was too young to know about life and death and danger.

Sarah took one last look down the road, then set Jenny on her feet and took her hand.

"Let's go back inside, Jenny. We have a lot of unpacking to do."

She led her daughter up the cracked sidewalk to the house she preferred to call "full of character" rather than dilapidated. With a fresh coat of paint and a thorough cleaning, it would be almost as good as new. She had been lucky to find it at such a good price. Her income was modest, and her child support payments were barely enough to pay for Jenny's clothes and schooling, let alone a fancy house.

Not that Sarah wanted to complain. Far from it. She had Jenny. And that was all that mattered.

The old screen door squeaked shut behind them. This time Sarah made sure it was latched. Jenny went straight to her toy box with her solemn dignified gait, then turned to smile at her mother as if to say, "What was all the fuss about?"

For a moment Sarah leaned her head against the

door frame and closed her eyes. Suddenly she felt very much alone and totally inadequate to the task of raising Jenny.

"Damn you, Bobby Wayne Love," she whispered. "Damn your selfish hide." The accusation, directed at her ex-husband, who was probably kicked back in a swivel chair in a car dealership somewhere in south Georgia, made her feel better. That's where the last few child support checks had come from, south Georgia; and Bobby Wayne had always been able to get a job selling. He was a smooth, fast talking man who could sell anything, including the notion that he would love Sarah Henley for better or for worse.

He hadn't survived the worst. Six months after Jenny's birth he had left. "I just can't cope," he had said.

Well, not only could Sarah cope, she could triumph. She straightened her shoulders and picked up her dust mop. She had a house to clean.

Jake pushed himself and his employees, confirming his reputation as a heartless machine. He strode through the Townsend Building like a hungry panther, growling orders here, changing magazine layouts there, sending employees scurrying on dozens of last-minute errands, driving himself until he was too exhausted to remember a pair of guileless blue eyes. And if he had been asked, he couldn't have told whether he was remembering Jenny's eyes or her mother's, the wise blue eyes of Sarah Love.

By late afternoon he knew he had to go back. He had to see for himself if Sarah and Jenny Love were all that he remembered.

He punched the intercom on his desk and paged his secretary. "Gwendolyn, will you come in here?"

When he called, Gwendolyn Phepps didn't waste time. She bustled into the office, glaring at him. Jake hid his smile. Gwendolyn was the only person at Townsend Publishing who was not afraid of him. She bullied him and he bullied her. Both of them loved it. And both of them pretended it was deadly serious.

"What took you so long, Gwendolyn?"

"It's Miss Phepps to you, Jake. And if you want somebody on roller skates, just say so, and I'll shagg my fanny out of here so fast, you won't see a thing except my dust. Now, dammit, what do you want?"

"You need to clean up your language, Miss Phepps. We're a serious publishing business around here."

"If we're all that serious, how come you wear ratty old blue jeans and shirts I wouldn't use for my dog's bedding and go squirting around on that motorcycle like a mad dog straight from hell?"

"You need to study syntax."

"You need to study manners."

Jake always let her have the last word. It was part of an unspoken pact between them. He twirled his gold pen between his fingers, watching it catch the late afternoon sunlight streaming through his sixth-floor office window.

Gwendolyn melted into an easy chair like butter on a hot bun, spreading her skirt around her enormous bulk. She looked totally relaxed. Jake wasn't fooled. Gwendolyn Phepps had the sharpness and energy of a rocket programmed to go to the moon.

"I don't have all day, you know," she reminded him.

"I'm thinking of ordering a rose," he said.

"A rose? You never order a rose. You always order orchids. And then never less than two dozen."

"This is different."

"How different?" He didn't answer. "One rose," she

continued. "It sounds personal to me, like you might finally be planning to join the land of the living."

"Gwendolyn, don't push your luck."

"No, sir." She saluted.

Jake twirled his pen again, watching the reflection of sunlight on his desk top and thinking of bright golden hair.

"Make it yellow," he said.

"What shall I put on the card?"

Jake mused awhile longer. He thought of Sarah Love with smudges on her rosy face. Of course, Sarah wasn't his concern. The child was the one he had scared half to death. "For Jenny," he said.

"Where shall I have the flower sent?"

"You know that old house on the edge of town? The one that's been vacant for so long?"

"Yes . . ." Gwendolyn bent her head over her pad as she wrote.

Jake imagined the delivery boy carrying the florist's box to the sagging old house. He imagined the look of surprise on Sarah Love's face. And Jenny . . . He couldn't imagine her reaction. She was unpredictable. Suddenly he wanted to see her reaction; he wanted to watch that angel's face as she caught her first glimpse of the yellow rose, just for her.

"Never mind," he said. "Just send it here."

Gwendolyn opened her mouth to comment, but Jake stood up and banged his palm on the desk. "Not another word, or I'll have you coated with peanut butter and hung out for the birds."

Jake decided to dress for the occasion. Though he generally stuck to jeans and comfortable clothes, except when he escorted one of the town's elegant beauties to a function that demanded formal clothes, he kept a wardrobe of suits and white shirts and proper ties at Townsend Publishing for those times when he needed to give the impression of being a conservative businessman whose only flash of the radical was an occasional fondness for wild ties. He also decided to drive his staid and steady Buick, parked in the company garage. He was afraid the motorcycle might bring back bad memories for the child.

He even caught himself whistling along with the radio once as he maneuvered the big car out of town; though why he should be so cheerful about calling on Jenny, he couldn't say. Nor could he fathom why he observed the speed limits—a first for him.

The gate leading up to the house was firmly pad-locked, so he parked the car by the side of the road. Not that it would have done any good to enter the gate: There was nothing but a path of weeds leading up to a garage that no longer had a roof. If Sarah Love had a car, she kept it hidden somewhere. Maybe her husband had driven it to work.

Jake realized he had never considered the possibility that Sarah Love might have a husband. He clutched his yellow rose while the dust settled on his white shirt, and speculated about the husband. He was probably somebody squat and square with a beer belly. Maybe he even chewed tobacco. Not that any of it mattered, of course. He hadn't come to see Sarah: he had come to see Jenny.

Tucking the rose under his arm, Jake climbed the fence. Though he hadn't climbed a fence in years, he still remembered how. When he was growing up, it had been a handy means of escape from the Townsend Mansion.

The sagging wooden steps creaked as he mounted them and rang the doorbell. There was no answer, no smiling face of Sarah Love, no patter of feet, no soft scurrying sounds or surreptitious straightening of furniture. Jake was undaunted. He had come to deliver a rose, and by George he was going to deliver it.

He left the porch and walked toward the backyard. Sarah was somewhere on the premises. Jake could sense her presence. All his senses were tingling, as if they were plugged into an electrical socket.

"Run, you fool," he muttered to himself. "Leave while there's still time."

He ignored his own warnings. Weeds pulled at his pants as he walked. Cockleburs caught in his socks. A lizard slithered over his shoes.

Unexpectedly he came upon them, Jenny and Sarah Love, sitting at a child's table in the middle of a weed patch, sipping from chipping china cups. They were having a tea party and had even dressed for the occasion. Jenny wore a white dress with a pink satin sash. A large bow, sagging slightly, held her wispy blond hair in place.

But it wasn't Jenny who held his attention: It was Sarah. No longer did she look as if she had come from an extended tour of duty in the desert. She wore a soft gauzy dress the color of ripe peaches. Her hair and skin shone as if they had been rubbed down with moon dust. And her face . . . Jake got lost in the contemplation of Sarah Love's face. It was heart-shaped, the features as delicate and rosy as if they had been sculpted from summer flowers. It was the kind of face men wrote poems about.

Watching them, he held his breath, unaware that he was squeezing the stem of the rose. He had come to a tumbledown house and stumbled into paradise. Sarah was smiling, and Jenny's laughter pealed on the warm summer air. Jake felt like an interloper, a stranger who had no business witnessing such innocent joy.

Once he had known the joy, heard the laughter, felt the warmth of a smile just for him. But he had destroyed the source, forfeited all rights. Watching the two at their private tea party, he felt like a thief.

Sarah's smile caught at his heart once more. He squeezed the rose and took a deep breath, forcing himself back in control.

He had merely come to deliver a flower. That was all. He decided to do it quickly before he took leave of his senses altogether.

Just when he was going to make his presence known, Sarah turned her head. Her smile wavered, then died. Her mouth formed a word, but no sound came out. For a fleeting moment Jake wondered what it would be like to kiss that mouth. Then he was furious with himself. He never wondered about women's mouths, he merely took them.

"Good afternoon," he said, sharper than he meant to. Sarah's eyes widened, and she reached for Jenny's hand. "I hope I didn't startle you."

Jake moved toward the pair at the small table, holding the rose in front of him to show his good intentions. "I brought a rose. . . ." Sarah's eyes held his. "For Jenny," he added.

"I'm so glad you came back." Sarah flashed her smile once more. He felt warmed. "You never told us your name, and I didn't know who to thank for . . ." She hesitated, swinging her gaze toward Jenny then back to him. ". . . this morning," she finished.

"Jake Townsend." He was beside the small table now, towering over it like some giant in a fairy tale, gazing down at two live princesses. Sarah and Jenny gave him twin smiles of almost dazzling radiance. Where was the absent Mr. Love? Why wasn't he there to protect these two lovely females?

"Jenny and I have worked so hard moving into our

new house, we decided to reward ourselves with a tea party. Won't you join us?" Sarah nodded toward a chair that wouldn't hold his left thigh, let alone all of him. He squatted beside the small table, an interloper, stealing what wasn't his.

"I don't want to intrude." It was a lie. He wanted desperately to intrude. He wanted to bask awhile longer in the warmth of Sarah's smile. "You're probably saving this place for your husband." He didn't know why it was suddenly important to know whether Sarah had a spouse. She was definitely not his type. All his playmates walked on the wild side. And certainly none of them had a child. *Never* a child.

"No." Some of the light went out of Sarah's face, but that was all she said.

There was no Mr. Love. Jake felt triumphant. Then he felt like a heel. Why should he be glad that two lovely and innocent females didn't have a protector?

"I'm sorry," he said, and he meant it.

"Don't be." Sarah brightened, and if her smile was false, Jake couldn't tell. "Jenny and I are a twosome. We like it that way."

"And I'm a loner." He smiled. "I like it that way." *Sometimes. When the dreams aren't too bad.* He kept smiling at Sarah, and somehow their gazes got tangled up and the summer air got heavy.

Sarah recovered first. "Why don't I get you a big chair? You look uncomfortable."

"No. I'm fine." He wasn't. He hadn't been fine in six years and didn't ever plan to be fine again. "Anyhow, I'm not staying long. I just came to deliver the rose."

He turned and handed the rose to Jenny. "This is for you, sweetheart."

Jenny didn't move.

"Go ahead, Jenny," her mother said. "The flower is for you."

Slowly Jenny reached for the rose. Her tiny hand closed around the petals and squeezed. "Pretty," she said. Her smile got big, and she stood up. "Pretty, pretty, pretty," she chanted. Then she marched solemnly through the weeds in ever-widening circles around the table, crushing the rose and chanting, "Pretty, pretty, pretty," in her faraway voice.

That was when Jake first knew that something was not right with Jenny. He wanted to gather the child to his chest and defend her with his life, and at the same time he wanted to run like hell.

"Jenny's special," her mother whispered.

"Yes, she certainly is." He hoped Sarah knew that he meant what he said.

"There is excellent training here for special children. That's why we came."

"I see."

"She has none of the outward signs of Down's syndrome. That's why she fools most people. Actually the doctors have never diagnosed her as a Down's child. They don't know why she's . . . special." Sarah folded and refolded the napkin in her lap. The sun shone on her golden hair. "I don't know why I'm telling you all this . . . except that you've been so kind." She lifted her eyes to him. They were very blue, and bright with sincerity. "And you're the only person I know in Florence."

"I'm sure you'll meet other people soon. Florence is filled with fine people."

Jake stood up to leave. Sarah didn't know him at all. And he didn't want her to find out. It was best to go while she still thought he was kind.

"You aren't leaving? I didn't even give you any tea."

Sarah stood beside him. The skirt of her flimsy summer dress drifted against his leg. He felt as if he had been touched by angels. Her light summer fragrance filtered into his senses. He felt as if he were drowning. Breathing became hard.

"Are you all right?" Sarah put her hand on his arm.

"Yes. I'm fine." He moved out of her reach. Jenny was still circling the weed patch, chanting. "Tell Jenny good-bye for me." He left quickly.

"Do come again," Sarah called after him.

He didn't breathe easy until he was sitting in his car. He would never come again. He had been a fool to come the first time.

He revved the engine to life and roared down the road, driving as if all the hounds of hell were in pursuit. He didn't stop until he reached the airport.

"Take me up," he yelled toward his friend Bert Donnogan, who was sitting outside the hangar where private planes were kept, his chair tilted back and a big cigar stuck in his mouth.

"Jake . . ." Bert jerked the unlit cigar from his mouth. "What the hell?"

"Just suit up and shut up, Bert. I'm going skydiving. And if you don't take me, I'll find somebody else who will."

Bert didn't argue.

An hour later they were over the target, a gentle rolling meadow. Bert circled once, twice, bringing the plane lower each time. When he was at thirteen thousand feet, he gave the signal.

Jake jumped. With arms spread and legs together in the swan-diving position, he fell through the sky.

"Twelve thousand, ten thousand, nine thousand," Bert whispered as he watched. Jake's body turned and spun, every movement beautifully controlled. There was nothing around him except miles and miles of blue sky.

When Jake reached two thousand feet, Bert yelled,

knowing he wouldn't be heard. "Now, dammit. Pull the rip cord now!"

Jake's body continued to float downward, the parachute neatly folded across his back. Sweat popped out on Bert's brow. He held his breath.

When Jake was pushing the limits, he slowly reached for the cord. The parachute unfolded like a giant cloud.

Bert wiped the sweat from his brow, muttering to himself, "Someday Jake Townsend is going to get himself killed."

Two

Jake's route to work took him by Sarah's raggedy yard and run-down house. He thought he could pass by, just as he always had. But he was wrong. Some powerful impulse made him turn his head and strain his eyes for a glimpse of golden hair, a flash of soft gauzy skirts, a fleeting glance of blue eyes.

He saw nothing except the house, accusing him with its ramshackle appearance.

Fool. Asking for trouble. He tightened his jaw. There was only one thing to do: Change his route to work. The new route took him fifteen minutes longer, but it was a price he was willing to pay for sanity.

"This is the third time this week you've been late, Jake." Gwendolyn stood in the middle of his office, hands propped on her hips. "You have about a million vices, but being late is not one of them."

"Is that any way to greet the boss, Gwendolyn? Aren't you afraid of getting fired?"

"Yes to the first question. No to the second. You

couldn't live without me, Jake." She plopped a stack of letters on his desk. "Sign these, then go in the bathroom and wash the road dust off your face and put on a suit. You have an appointment with Mr. High-and-Mighty himself." She was referring to their least favorite client, H. L. Clevenger.

"Gwendolyn, someday you're going to forget yourself and call Froggy that to his face, and then we'll lose a big account."

"My mind's a steel trap. I never forget, which is not to say the same for you. One of these days you're going to call him Froggy, and I'm going to be standing behind the door laughing my head off."

"You're warped."

"That's why you love me. Go wash your face."

Jake signed the papers then went into the bathroom, cupped his hands under the faucet, and splashed water on his face. Reaching for the towel, he caught a glimpse of himself in the mirror. The water looked like tears. He leaned closer and watched the moisture stream down his cheeks. *Tears—and a blue-eyed child who had called him Daddy.*

"I never forget either, Gwendolyn. Never," he whispered.

The blue eyes haunted him all day. By late afternoon he was so exhausted, he couldn't remember whether the blue eyes were a part of his past or a part of his present. All he knew was that he felt empty and cowardly.

Sarah and Jenny Love were two people in need, without a soul in Florence to call friend. Would it kill him to do a small kindness? Surely he had that much humanity left in him.

He punched the intercom. "Gwendolyn, I need you."

"You and every other handsome stud in Florence.

Can this wait, Jake? You've run me ragged today, and I'm having a well-deserved cup of coffee."

"No, it can't wait, Gwendolyn. Bring your coffee with you."

"This is bad for my digestion, you know." Gwendolyn settled herself in the most comfortable chair, being careful not to spill coffee.

"Gwendolyn, does Townsend Publishing own a lawn mower?"

"We own one, but I don't think it's nearly as fast as that motorcycle you ride. Are you planning to add yardwork to your list of ways to get yourself killed?"

"It's none of your business what I'm planning to do. Just tell me where the damned thing is."

"Down in the garage beside Newt Thompson's pickup truck. But if you're planning on using it, you'd best be advised to ask Newt's permission. He's mighty possessive about his equipment."

"I own everything in Townsend Enterprises, including the damned lawn mower."

"Nevertheless, if you want to keep a good maintenance man, you'd better ask Newt."

Jake scowled at her, mainly because he knew she'd be disappointed if he didn't. They had to keep up appearances. It wouldn't do if either of them slipped up and let on how important they were to each other.

"All the sweet-talking secretaries in Florence, and I had to hire Attila the Hun."

"I'm not a secretary; I'm an executive assistant, and don't you forget that, Jake." Gwendolyn glared at him over the rim of her coffee cup, then flounced out.

He chuckled, but not until after the door had closed behind her. Then he went downstairs to ask Newt Thompson if he could borrow his own lawn mower.

• • •

Sarah stood on her front porch batting a red balloon with Jenny. Jenny loved bright colors, and batting the balloon helped her with coordination. It was one of the things Sarah had discovered on her own. All Jenny's doctors and teachers had been good, but they didn't have Sarah's determination or her faith. The doctors had said Jenny might never walk. Sarah and Jenny had proved them wrong. They had said she was capable of making sounds, but she might never be able to organize those sounds into words—and certainly not sentences. Jenny would never give the valedictory address at her high-school graduation, but she could definitely talk. Sarah had seen to that.

"Mine, mine, mine," Jenny chanted, meaning *Mommy, you've held the balloon too long. Quit daydreaming and send it to me.*

Laughing, Sarah batted the balloon toward her impatient daughter. The late afternoon sun turned the balloon into a sparkling jewel.

"Pretty, pretty, pretty," Jenny chanted, batting at the balloon and missing. She fell onto her bottom and gave her mother a look of such wounded dignity that Sarah had to bite her lip to keep from laughing.

"Let me give you a hand up, Jenny."

"No. Me." Jenny pushed her hand away and stuck out her lower lip. "ME!"

Sarah watched Jenny's great struggle as she tried to get her body to cooperate with her strong will. In four years of fighting for every small victory, Jenny had learned great perseverance and Sarah had learned patience.

"Come on, Jenny. You can do it."

"Yes. ME! ME!"

"Come on Jenny! That's my girl." Sarah clapped and urged her daughter on. "That's my big brave girl."

They were making such a racket, neither of them heard the sound of a motor.

"Hey! Anybody home?"

Sarah recognized the voice immediately. Feeling flushed and breathless, she turned toward her front gate. There was Jake Townsend, as big as she remembered and far more handsome, sitting on a lawn mower, of all things. His shirt sleeves were rolled up, he had dust all over his face, and his wild black hair was so tousled, he looked as if he had just returned from a windy climb down Mount McKinley.

"Oh." She pressed her hand over her heart.

"Did I scare you?" He got off the lawn mower, and she would swear he looked as if he were dismounting a magnificent stallion.

Sarah was so flustered, she forgot all about Jenny's struggle to get off the porch floor.

"Why, no. You didn't scare me," she called. "I was startled. That's all." She patted her hair, though what good it would do at this stage of the game, she had no idea. She probably looked like a frazzled, overworked shop girl. She wished she had combed her hair before she'd come out to the porch. It felt all wispy around her face.

"Do you think you might undo the latch so I can get this trusty steed through the gate?"

Sarah felt like a giddy schoolgirl. Here she was worrying about her hair, and Jake Townsend was standing in the road. Land sakes, her manners around men were as rusty as they could be. Not that it mattered, for she had neither the time nor the heart for men. But Jake wasn't just any man. He had saved Jenny's life.

"Just a minute." Sarah snatched Jenny off the porch. It wouldn't do to leave her alone, even while she went the short distance to the gate. In that length of time Jenny was perfectly capable of disappearing altogether. Sometimes she was that fast.

"No!" Jenny said. "Me, me, me."

"Shhh. Hush darling." Sarah smoothed Jenny's hair as she headed toward the latched gate. "Our friend is here. The nice man who brought you the flower."

Jenny looked at her visitor, and her face bloomed with joy. "Nice man."

"Hello, Jenny." Jake Townsend reached over the gate and took Jenny's hand.

All that was well and good, of course, but Sarah was busy with the gate and holding Jenny all at the same time. Things got complicated when Jake's arm brushed against hers. The shock of the contact rendered her helpless. Her hands got clumsy and the latch got uncooperative.

"Need any help there? I can climb over and undo it for you." Jake released Jenny's hand, and thankfully Sarah got back to normal. How silly she was acting over Jenny's friend.

"No." She even managed a smile. "I'll have it open in a jiffy."

He smiled back at her, and oh, she hadn't remembered how green his eyes were. She got lost in the contemplation of them. Jake's eyes were so green and so beautiful—and so very empty, as if the man behind them didn't live there anymore. The sad emptiness reached out and touched Sarah in ways she had never been touched. *Who are you, Jake Townsend?* her mind whispered. *And how did you climb so quickly into my heart?*

She was being silly, of course. Jake hadn't climbed

into her heart at all. She was missing her old friends back in Birmingham. That was all. She was lonely.

She concentrated on the gate and tried not to feel Jake's gaze upon her. Some men had ways of looking at a woman that made her feel touched. Jake was one of them. Sarah could feel his gaze upon her, and everywhere it touched, her skin felt warm and tingly.

She hugged Jenny closer and concentrated on the latch. Stubborn old thing. It finally gave way, but not before Sarah said a word.

"Well, fiddlesticks." She looked up at Jake. He was suppressing a smile.

"Sometimes gates can be stubborn," he said. Then he walked into her overgrown yard like some prince out of a fairy tale and stood tall and handsome, as if he were surveying his kingdom. "It was a spur-of-the-moment decision, coming here like this, assuming you would allow me to help you with the mowing." He smiled down at her. "I hope you don't mind."

"It's kind of you." She shifted Jenny's weight to her other hip and tried not to take Jake's smile personally. Just because his smile made her feel as if it were all for her benefit didn't mean he had one iota of interest in her. Not one. Which was all well and good, for she certainly had her hands full with Jenny.

"Please don't be mistaken about me, Sarah. I'm neither kind nor generous, but since you're new in town and I had this perfectly good lawn mower sitting in the garage at Townsend Publishing, I thought I'd come out and lend you a hand." He smiled. "The real pity is that I didn't have a truck to haul it in. Newt wouldn't let me borrow the truck."

"Who's Newt?"

"My maintenance man. He was skeptical enough about letting me use the mower. He had grave doubts that I could operate it."

Sarah laughed. "Can you?"

"Lady, I can drive anything on wheels."

Sarah felt bright and giddy, caught up in Jake's laughter like a red balloon in the sunshine. She tipped her head back, laughing. And Jenny laughed with her. She sensed Jake's eyes studying her again, and they felt so very good. *Sarah, Sarah,* she chided herself. *This man has come to mow the lawn. That's all.*

"I'm afraid I can't pay you right now," she said, sobering suddenly.

"This is not for pay, Sarah. It's . . . for Jenny."

"Well, in that case . . . Jenny is so pleased. And so am I." She offered her hand. "Thank you." He held her hand so briefly, she might have imagined the touch. But she had proof. Her skin still tingled.

"Me, me, me." Jenny pointed at the mower.

"No, darling. You can't ride. It's too dangerous. But we will watch from the porch."

"Stand well back," Jake said. "The mower might sling a stick. And hold tight to Jenny."

Sarah climbed the porch with her daughter, then settled into a straight-back chair with Jenny in her lap. Someday she hoped to get a porch swing, but for now she was content with her chair.

She hummed to Jenny as Jake began to mow her scraggly lawn. Every time he passed in front of the porch, he waved and smiled. Jenny waved back. Sarah felt like waving, but she thought that might look too obvious. It was wonderful to have a man taking care of her yard. All week she had wondered how she would get the yardwork done. She couldn't afford to hire someone, and she certainly couldn't afford a mower.

Back in Birmingham she had learned to swap

services for yardwork. She had done some baking for one of her neighbors who sometimes mowed. She had exchanged some of her handmade dolls for the services of another. He had many grandchildren and claimed he would use them all for presents, though sometimes Sarah believed he was just being kind. People were often kind to her and Jenny. It made her believe in the basic goodness of man.

"Nice man," Jenny said, waving as Jake passed by.

"Yes, darling. He's a very nice man. His name is Jake."

"'ake?"

"That's right. Jake. Can you say Jake?" She enunciated carefully, emphasizing the *J*.

"'ake," Jenny said, proud of herself.

Some sounds were too difficult for Jenny, and she dropped them. *It will all come in time* Sarah told herself.

The mower passed by again, with Jake sitting in the driver's seat like a Roman gladiator, waving to his biggest fans from his chariot.

"He actually seems to be enjoying this," she mused aloud.

"'ake?" Jenny asked, as if she understood perfectly what her mother meant.

Sarah hugged her close. "Oh, Jenny. Jenny. How much do you know in that bright little mind of yours? What wonderful insights are trapped by your inability to communicate?"

"'ake?" Jenny shrugged her shoulders and held her hands out, palms up, in the eloquent gesture Sarah knew so well. "'ere?"

"Where is Jake, my darling? He's gone to the backyard to mow. Let's go inside and make him some gingerbread." Jenny studied her mother solemnly as if she doubted the wisdom of Sarah's suggestion. "Gingerbread boys for Jake."

"Yes," Jenny said.

The yard was finished. Jake was dusty and sweaty, and bits of grass clung to his arms; but he couldn't remember when he had felt happier.

"If doing good deeds is this exhilarating, I'll have to take it up as a hobby," he announced to a robin in the oak tree behind Sarah's house.

He surveyed his handiwork, proud of himself. Newt would have to eat his words. There wasn't a thing wrong with the yard that a little edging and trimming wouldn't cure.

"Next time I'll bring the edger," he said, thinking aloud. His own words brought him up short. There might not be a next time. He hadn't made up his mind about that.

He brushed the grass off his arms and started to the house to tell Sarah the yard was finished. That's when he smelled gingerbread. He stood in the middle of the yard with his head tipped back, sniffing. Gingerbread. Memories flooded over him.

" *Daddy! Daddy! Can I have the heads?*"

"*Of course you can have the heads, sweetheart. Daddy likes the feet.*"

"*Goody. I like to eat the smiles.*"

Bonnie smiled at him and hugged him hard. "*I love you best in all the world, Daddy.*"

"I love you, too, Bonnie," he whispered. "I will always love you."

"The yard looks wonderful." Jake passed his hands over his eyes. Sarah Love was standing at the backdoor. Jenny stood beside her, smiling at him from behind her mother's skirt. "I don't know what I would have done if you hadn't come along to mow it."

Mother and child, standing at the backdoor with the setting sun sparking their hair golden. They looked as if they were wearing halos. Twin angels. The spicy smell of gingerbread drifted through the open door.

"Jenny and I made gingerbread."

"It smells delicious."

"It's for you."

Sarah's face glowed from the heat of the stove. Or perhaps it was from her innocence. She looked so innocent standing in the doorway offering him gingerbread. A saint consorting with a sinner. What would she do if she knew he had killed his wife and daughter?"

"I really shouldn't stay," he said.

"Oh." He could see the disappointment on Sarah's face. Women sought him out, vied for his attention, even lusted after him; but none cared enough to be *disappointed* when he decided to leave. Standing in the backyard watching Sarah, seeing the genuine concern in her face, Jake felt his dark heart expand.

Leave, his mind said, even as his heart said *stay.*

"Perhaps I can stay a little while."

"That will be lovely." Sarah held the door wide. She was wearing a sweet smelling perfume that invaded his senses. Jake was careful not to brush against her as he passed through. Still, the fragrance of summer flowers settled over him like a blessing.

The kitchen was high ceilinged and spacious but sparsely furnished. A simple stove and refrigerator, both old, stood in one corner. The table was old, too, but shining with furniture polish. A multicolor braided rug relieved the tedium of a cracked linoleum floor. In the center of the table stood a pottery jar filled with wildflowers—Queen Anne's lace and black-eyed Susans.

"Please make yourself at home." Sarah gestured toward the table and chairs. "I'll get you a glass of lemonade. You must be so hot."

"Yes, I'm hot," Jake said, and meant it in more ways than one. Sarah looked cool and delicious moving about her kitchen. Gracious and charming. Inviting and approachable. In fact, she was by far the most appealing woman he had ever met. But not once did he think of making a play for her. Sarah Love was not the kind of woman a man took lightly. She was not the kind a man could wine and dine and forget. And she was certainly not the kind to grace a man's sheets and not his heart.

Jake's palms got sweaty and his blood roared through his veins. Sarah Love was the most *dangerous* woman he had ever met.

"Here you are. Nice and cool."

She offered him the lemonade, smiling. Their hands touched, hers sweet and soft, his hot and sweaty. Her eyes widened, then got bright in the center. He held her gaze. The ice melted in the glass and cracked apart with a small pop. It might have been his heart melting, melting under the influence of Sarah's blue eyes and her sweet touch.

She stepped out of his reach, self-conscious. She lifted her hand and fussed with her hair. The gesture was feminine and endearing. Jake couldn't stop watching her.

"My." Her voice sounded breathless. "I do love lemonade in the kitchen on a warm summer evening." She tucked a shiny curl behind her ear. "Kitchens are so cozy, don't you think? This one will be even nicer when I get some curtains made."

He breathed deeply, trying to concentrate on what

she was saying instead of what she was—an angel in disguise.

"You sew?"

"Why yes." Her smile was radiant, as if she had just won the Nobel Peace Prize: "It's my profession, actually. I make dolls. Jenny helps me."

"I've never met a dollmaker. Tell me how you do it." He really wanted to know. But more than that, he wanted to keep Sarah by his side, talking in her musical voice, fussing with her shiny hair.

Sarah sat in the chair opposite him and explained dollmaking. Jenny stood on a stool at the cabinet, humming to herself and occasionally pausing to say, "Good."

"Two stores in Birmingham and one in Atlanta carry my dolls. I'll set up a shop here in the house. It's perfect—so much light and space." She paused, flushed.

Jake wanted to touch her rosy face. He wanted to put his finger on her lips and trace their heart-shaped outline.

"The best part about the dolls is that Jenny helps. She paints the faces."

"Jenny paints?"

"Yes. Because of her compensatory and extraordinary talent, doctors call her an idiot savant. I've never liked that term." Some of the glow left Sarah's face, and her eyes became troubled. "I prefer to think of her as merely having a special gift. She puts the heart and soul into the dolls."

"Good," Jenny chanted from the other side of the kitchen. "Good, good, good."

"The gingerbread." Sarah jumped from her chair and hurried to Jenny's side. "Oh, Jenny." Sarah lifted a mutilated gingerbread boy off the tray. "Oh, honey."

"Good!" Jenny turned to smile at Jake. Gingerbread crumbs decorated her mouth.

"I was enjoying our conversation so much, I forgot about her." Sarah helped Jenny off the stool, then lifted the tray and brought it to the table. It was filled with gingerbread boys, all of them without heads. "She likes the heads."

Daddy, can I have the heads?

Jake gripped the edge of the table. Time spun backward, and he felt dizzy.

"I hope you don't mind." Sarah pressed a headless cookie into his hand.

Jake fought for control and won. He even managed a smile.

"No. I've always been partial to feet." He forced himself to sit in the chair facing four-year-old Jenny with Bonnie's blue eyes, and eat two gingerbread boys. "These are very good, sweetheart. Did you help make them?"

"Yes. Me, me, me."

"You're a smart little girl." He took another bite. "Mmm, good."

Jenny laughed. *I love you best in all the world, Daddy.*

"You have a way with children," Sarah said.

"Thank you," he said, standing. He felt smothered, trapped. "I really must be going."

"Oh." Sarah stood beside him, so close, he could have reached out and touched her. He leaned forward. She was alive, real. He needed her. Time stretched out, shimmering between them, poignant as a memory, breathless as a promise.

"I was going to invite you to dinner," Sarah added. "I made pot roast."

"Another time, perhaps." It was a narrow escape. If she hadn't spoken, he might have put his hand on the smooth, firm flesh of her upper arm. He might have pulled her close and buried his face in the creamy inviting space between her slender neck and her soft shoulder.

He hurried toward the door. With his hand on the screen, he remembered. "I left a patch of wildflowers," he said over his shoulder. "For Jenny. Sometimes late in the evening, fireflies come."

Sarah was saying something, but he didn't hear. He burst through the door and breathed deeply. It was already dark outside with only a few early stars and one single firefly to light his way to the lawn mower. He climbed aboard.

Riding the lawn mower five miles back to the Townsend Building in the dark hadn't been his original plan. But neither was falling under Sarah Love's spell.

He turned the key, and the mower roared to life. He had planned to leave the mower for Newt to pick up the next day, then call a taxi to take him back into town. All those plans were scrapped.

He thought of rushing through the gate and never looking back, but then he remembered the first time he'd seen Jenny, standing in the middle of the road with her thumb in her mouth. Cursing, he went into the yard, latched the gate, climbed back over the fence, and back onto his lawn mower. Then he started down the dark highway, breaking the law. Driving an unauthorized vehicle on a public road.

"It's a damned fool thing to do. Driving a lawn mower through town. Who do I think I am, anyhow? Some damned hero?" He clenched his jaw hard enough to break teeth. "Newt would have done it. Hell, all I had to do was ask him."

Sarah's face, rosy with heat, floated into his vision. Jake gripped the steering wheel, cursing the slowness of his machine. Five ridiculous-damn-fool miles per hour.

He was in a black fury by the time he reached the Townsend Building. He left the mower in the garage and rode the elevator upstairs to his office. He was jerking his clothes off by the time he got through his door. They made a messy trail behind him.

A shower. That's what he needed. Something to cool him off.

He stepped in, still wearing his socks, then tipped his face up. The water hit him full force, so cold, it brought chill bumps all over his body. Sarah's face came to him, sweet and inviting.

What he needed was a good strong antidote. He finished his shower quickly, then hurried to his phone, wearing a large towel around his waist and wet socks on his feet.

He hit the jackpot on the first try.

"Denise?"

"Jake? Sweetie, is that you?"

"Yes." She was glad to hear from him. How long had it been since he had last called her? Three weeks? Four? "Are you free?"

"For you, Jake, always."

"I'll be there in thirty minutes."

"The door will be open."

Jake cradled the phone. Denise was going to rescue him. He jerked a clean shirt and pants out of his closet. Funny, he didn't feel rescued; he felt tarnished. He was going to use one woman to forget another, blackhearted bastard that he was. What did one more sin matter?

He hurried toward the door, then turned back to pick up his clothes. No use in setting himself up for Gwendolyn. She would have plenty to say to him as it was—driving a lawn mower through the streets, mowing a yard for people he barely knew.

Except he knew the light in Sarah's eyes. He knew the music of her voice.

Jake threw the clothes onto the bathroom floor and slammed the door shut. He needed Denise.

She was waiting for him inside her modern apartment. All the surfaces were black and white, hard and shiny. Even Denise looked hard and shiny, backlit by a gooseneck white lamp, her straight black hair and black gown stark in the dim glow.

He walked straight to her and pulled her into his arms. She fitted her body to his. For a moment he studied her face, searching for a rosy glow, a pair of heart-shaped lips, a pair of bright and shining eyes. Denise's black eyes absorbed the light, swallowed it up.

He bent over her quickly, before he could change his mind. Her kiss was expert, eager. He told himself she was exactly what he needed.

Denise broke off the kiss and leaned back to look at him. "You're tense, Jake. Tired?"

"Yes. I'm tired."

"I'll fix that." She caught his hand and led him toward the bedroom. Her silk gown brushed against his leg.

The sun glinted on golden hair. A filmy peach-color skirt whispered against his leg. Memories. Jake passed his hand over his face. Would he never be rid of memories?

Denise was shedding her gown. Both straps hung over her shoulders. Her skin was lightly tanned, baked that way in a machine that looked like a coffin.

He reached out to touch her. Denise was smooth,

hard, firm. He splayed his fingers across her shoulders, feeling the warm soft skin of Sarah Love.

"Damn." He drew his hand back.

"Jake?"

"I'm sorry, Denise." *You're the wrong woman.* "I guess I'm too tired after all."

Denise cupped his face, pulling it down close to hers. "That's all right, Jake." She gave him a friendly kiss on his chin. "Don't be a stranger, sweetie."

He patted her cheek. "You deserve a good man, Denise."

"You are a good man, Jake."

He left quickly. Denise had rescued him, all right, but not from Sarah Love: she had rescued him from a potentially embarrassing situation. He would always be grateful. But he wouldn't call her again. She deserved better treatment.

She was more than a beautiful, efficient love machine. She had a heart and feelings and dreams. He was wrong to try to use her to hold back his ghosts with one careless hour of forgetfulness.

He climbed on his motorcycle and drove home, pursued by his demons—past and present.

Three

Jake had all day Saturday to brood over his sins—which were legion. The first thing he did was order three dozen orchids for Denise and send them to her house along with a card that said, "Sorry about last night. Find happiness with a good man. Jake." Then he rode his motorcycle into the bluffs along the Tennessee River that snaked through the Quad Cities of Florence, Sheffield, Muscle Shoals, and Tuscumbia.

He drove too fast and too close to the edge of the bluffs, defying fate, challenging death, hoping the motorcycle would plunge into the dark river far below, willing the roaring waters to carry him into oblivion—and breathing a prayer of relief when he was spared. Hour after hour he tempted fate and won.

Finally, feeling hollow and isolated, he parked his powerful machine under a centuries-old oak, then walked to the edge of the bluff and stood watching the river. Water, so much water. It had been raining the night he lost Bonnie. *Lost her. Killed her.*

"Nooo." He gave voice to his agony. Kneeling beside the river, he relived the horrible night she had died. He held her in his arms, a fragile and broken blue-eyed doll. *I love you best in all the world, Daddy,* she'd whispered. And then she was gone.

Nothing could alter the facts. His daughter was dead and he was alive. No matter how fast he ran, he could never outrun the guilt.

Wearily he climbed back onto his motorcycle and drove back into town, this time without speeding. He had already turned onto the road that led back to his house when he found himself making a U-turn. As if it knew the way, the motorcycle meandered to the far side of town until he was on Sarah's road.

He didn't try to understand what drew him there, but he did make a plan of sorts. He would merely drive by to see how the yard looked. If he caught a glimpse of Sarah and Jenny, he would wave, just to let them know they had a friend in town.

When he saw Sarah, all his plans fell by the wayside. She was walking up the dusty road, leading Jenny with one hand and carrying a big sack in the other. The weight of the sack pulled her sideways, so that she walked tilted to the left.

Jake stopped his motorcycle atop the hill and watched from a distance. No use getting involved, he thought. But even at a distance Sarah pulled at his heart. There was something brave about the way she walked, something noble and good. It might have been the lift of her chin or the spring in her step or the determined look on her face.

Jake squinted into the evening sun in order to get a better look at her. Bits of sunset were caught in her hair, streaks of red and gold, so that she seemed to be wearing a crown from Tiffany's.

As he watched, Sarah bent over to pick up Jenny,

and the sack she was carrying burst open. Two cans went rolling down the road.

Jake put the motorcycle in gear and roared off, coming to a careful stop beside Sarah Love. He had meant to say something casual about rescuing two damsels in distress, but one look at Sarah's face and he forgot everything. A fine powdering of road dust turned her skin dark, and her eyes shone forth like twin beacons, reflecting the sun. He got lost in the brilliance of her blue eyes.

She dropped her torn sack and smoothed back a lock of hair that had fallen over her forehead, never taking her eyes off him. Sarah, so proud, covered with dust from the road because she didn't have a car—or a husband to take care of her.

Jake silently cursed his own selfishness. He had spent the day in frivolity while Sarah walked the road with her heavy sack and her special child.

"Oh . . . I didn't expect to see you," she said, smiling and patting her hair, as if he had just rung her doorbell and she were welcoming him into her parlor.

"Do you need some help?" Foolish question, but her eyes had bewitched him.

"I guess the bag got too heavy." She looked down at her broken sack. "And my paint is making a fast getaway toward Florence."

Jake jumped off his bike and raced after the runaway paint cans. He caught up with them just before they rolled into a ditch.

He glanced at the labels. Wedgwood blue, latex, and ivory, satin finish enamel. Sarah was going to paint one of her rooms. Which one? Her bedroom?

A vision of Sarah in a freshly painted bedroom rose up in Jake's mind. He tried to run away from it by hurrying up the hill toward her.

"They were ornery," he said, "but I subdued them."

"Thank you," Sarah said, smiling and reaching for the cans.

"It looks as if you have your hands full. I'll take the paint to the house for you."

"We've taken up too much of your time already."

"No. You've rescued me from a lonely Saturday evening." It was a confession he hadn't meant to make, but once he'd said it, he realized it was true.

"And you've rescued me," she said, so softly he had to bend close to hear.

"'ake!" Suddenly Jenny held out her arms to him. "Me!"

"Oh, my." Laughing, Sarah tried to hold on to her struggling daughter. "Jake can't carry you and the paint, Jenny. Be a good girl now and stop wiggling."

"She wants me to take her?"

"I'm afraid so. I guess I've spoiled her."

"Me!" Jenny demanded, still holding her arms toward him. She tipped her chin up and stuck out her lower lip. "Me!"

"I'm afraid she doesn't accept defeat easily," Sarah explained.

"Why should she?" Jake set the paint cans beside the road and reached for Jenny. She felt as fragile as a rose. She caught his face between his hands and rubbed her tiny nose against his.

"Nice man."

"Yes, he is, darling. He's a very nice man."

He felt a terrible aching in the dark recesses of his soul. At that moment he would have given everything he owned to be the nice man Sarah and Jenny Love thought he was.

Jenny's soft hair brushed his cheek, and flowers bloomed in his soul. He smiled down at Jenny, then at Sarah.

"Have you ever ridden a motorcycle?"

"Why, no."

"Then let's all climb aboard, and I'll take you home . . . if you aren't afraid."

"Will we all fit?"

"You can ride behind me, Jenny in front. I'll come back for the paint."

"Jenny will love that."

They climbed aboard his motorcycle. Jake held Jenny, who was squealing with delight, and Sarah sat behind him.

"You'll have to put your arms around my waist, Sarah. Otherwise I might lose you."

She circled his waist. It was a light touch, but it transported him. His spirit threw off the dark shackles of the past and lifted into the sky, higher and higher until he touched the setting sun, absorbed all the colors, red and gold and purple, so that he glowed. All because of Sarah's touch.

Jake closed his eyes, knowing she couldn't see. *What about you, Sarah? Do you love this? Sitting so close, your body pressed into my back?*

"Jake? Are we ready?"

Sarah's soft question brought Jake back to earth.

"We're ready. Hold on tight."

When he put the machine into motion, Sarah's hold tightened. He wanted to ride forever, ride off into the sunset with his stolen bounty, a child who reminded him of Bonnie and a woman who reminded him of love.

But they didn't belong to him. He didn't want them to belong to him. He was careless. He broke things. He broke people.

He kicked the machine into motion and drove with great caution up the hill. Sarah's house was in sight. He didn't have far to go with his precious packages.

Just a short distance, and he could deliver them safely.

Sarah squeezed his waist. She flattened her cheek against his back, and he could feel her warm breath through his shirt. The house loomed closer.

Jake began to sweat. Would a car come barreling down the road, taking the curve too fast? Would it smash into them, killing Jenny first, then Sarah? His hands trembled on the handlebars. Silently he prayed. *Just this once. Let me be a protector. Just this once.*

By the time he reached Sarah's gate he was in need of a good stiff drink. She dismounted and reached for Jenny.

"That was exhilarating, Jake. I've never ridden a motorcycle."

"I'm glad you liked it."

Behind her coating of dust, Sarah glowed. *Don't like me too much, Sarah. Don't trust me*, his inner voice warned.

"I'll go back for the paint," he said, turning abruptly away so she couldn't see his face. He waited until they were through the gate before he left.

The engine roared in his ears and the wind whistled around him. He was empty. No sweet arms wrapped his waist, no soft cheek pressed his back. He was alone.

Jenny wanted to stay and watch the motorcycle, but Sarah hurried into the house. She wanted to wash the dust off her face before Jake came back. Call it pride. Call it silly vanity. Every time she saw Jake she looked like a bag lady.

"Let's hurry, Jenny. Let's get pretty for Jake."

When she reached the bathroom, she handed

Jenny a brush to occupy herself, then hastily washed her face. Would she have time to apply lipstick? She decided yes.

Her hands shook. What was there about Jake Townsend that made her feel so warm and shaky inside? Here she was, primping like a silly schoolgirl. Sarah smiled and kept on primping. She was just tucking her last stray curl out of sight when the doorbell rang.

She pressed her hand over her heart. "My goodness," she said, flustered. She absently smoothed her hand through her hair, causing the stray curl to come loose and curve against her cheek.

"'ake," Jenny screamed, then trotted toward the door in her brave rolling gait.

Jake was standing on her front porch with her paint cans, backlit by the setting sun. He looked like one of those heroes in Westerns who always appeared sitting atop a huge horse.

"Where's your horse?" she blurted out.

"I beg your pardon?"

Sarah was mortified. Here he was, an important businessman—she knew because she'd inquired in town about his work—and here she was, a woman always depending on the kindness of strangers, like Blanche in *A Streetcar Named Desire*. He was going to think she was flirting with him. Or worse, he was going to catch on to the idea that she had enjoyed every blessed minute of that motorcycle ride because she had liked being pressed up against his broad warm back.

There now, she had finally admitted it. She *had* liked it. Furthermore, it felt good to see Jake on her front porch holding her paint cans. Sometimes she got so tired of doing every little thing for herself, she didn't know what to do. Not that she would change a thing, and not that she wanted to complain . . .

"I do have horses," Jake said, smiling, "but not with me."

Sarah patted her hair. "I was just being silly. You reminded me of one of those heroes in the Westerns who never seem to be without a horse."

"I remind you of a hero?" Jake seemed pleased with the idea.

"Well . . . yes."

He smiled at her, and she smiled back, and they kept on grinning at each other that way through the half-open screen door. Then Jenny got loose from Sarah's hand and wrapped herself around Jake's leg. His smile wobbled, like one of those spinning tops about to wind down.

"Jenny. Come here, darling."

"No!"

"Let the nice man alone. He's brought our paint and he has to go."

"No! Want 'ake."

Sarah's heart broke a little as she watched her small daughter clinging to Jake's leg. She wanted Jake too. She wanted his calm presence. She wanted him to fill a room as only a big man could. She wanted to lean on his broad shoulders. She wanted to share small day-to-day problems with him. But, oh, most of all she wanted him to make the loneliness go away.

Oh, she was as selfish as the day was long, standing in the setting sun thinking of her own needs when her daughter's needs were so great. Dear sweet Jenny with all her special ways. Her own father hadn't been able to cope. What man in his right mind would willingly embrace the task of taking care of

Jenny? Sarah had best quit dreaming and settle for reality.

"Come, Jenny," she said, bending down to peel her daughter away.

"Don't. It's all right." Jake squatted beside her and caught her hand. Sarah could have stayed that way forever with her hand nestled in his. She felt protected, cherished, though why such a small gesture should make her feel that way, she couldn't say. Nor could she say why his leg brushing against her set her aflame. She guessed it had been too long since she had attended to her own needs. Not that there was anybody around to attend to them, and not that she was looking. But Jake . . .

"Why don't I come inside?" Jake smiled at her. She was sorry when he took his hand away. "That is . . . if you don't mind."

"Mind? Why, that's a lovely idea."

"I'll bring Jenny." Jake lifted her daughter and carried her into the house. Jenny looked as if she had just discovered Christmas, and Sarah felt as if she were glowing herself.

Jake brought Jenny into the den—thank goodness she'd had time to get it in order. Then he stood there looking uncertain.

Sarah was puzzled. One minute Jake was perfectly at ease, laughing and talking, and the next he was as closed and untouchable as if he had gone off to Alaska without telling anybody.

She guessed he was tired of being put upon by a helpless female. Of course, Sarah was far from helpless, but lately she must have appeared that way, especially to a stranger. Well, almost a stranger.

"Come, Jenny." Striving to be brisk and efficient but not rude, she reached for her daughter. "We've taken up far too much of Jake's time."

"Not at all." He looked relieved to be rid of his burden. Dreams that had been springing to life inside her heart like wild summer flowers suddenly wilted. Why should Jake have to cope with Jenny? Why would he want to? Jenny's own father hadn't been able to stand the pressure.

"Actually, I was beginning to enjoy my role of hero," Jake added.

"You were?" Sarah studied the quicksilver man standing beside her. The casual observer might have said he was smiling, but Sarah wasn't a casual observer. She was seeing with her heart. There was a look of such poignancy on his face, she wanted to take him into her arms. She wanted to rock him and croon to him. She wanted to be balm to his soul, succor for his spirit.

Ah, Sarah, Sarah, she chided herself. *This will never do.*

"It isn't often a man is called upon to be a hero," he said.

"I need a hero daily." The words slipped out before Sarah could stop them. That was not the kind of admission she wanted to make to this complex man. "What I mean is . . ."

"I understand," he said gently, bending closer to her.

"No." She set Jenny down and was only vaguely aware of her daughter's dignified exit to the toy box. "It's not that my burdens are too great or that I feel unequal to the task. Far from it. I'm strong. I'm perfectly able to take care of Jenny." She pushed at her hair. Her face felt hot. She guessed she was overdoing the defensive bit, but she would not show any weakness before Jake Townsend. "Jenny and I have a wonderful life together. Really, we do."

"Sarah. I know you're strong and brave." Jake

reached for her hand. She felt as if she had been sucked into the center of an electrical storm. "And I can see that you have a wonderful life."

"You can?"

"Yes. Where there is this much love in a house, life has to be wonderful." Did she hear a note of longing in his voice, or was she transferring her own feelings to him?

"Thank you. That's a beautiful thing to say." He still held her hand. She didn't want him to let go. "You are truly kind."

"Don't." He dropped her hand and turned his back to her.

"Jake." She put her hand on his back. Jake stiffened with tension. She felt the tightening of his muscles underneath his shirt. "Why do you turn away from compliments?"

He stood, silent and tense. Sarah thought he might leave without another word. Finally he turned back to her. His face was tight.

"Show me the paintbrushes and the room you want painted."

"Why?" He was changing the subject, and she wasn't quite willing to let the old one go.

"Call it a mutual rescue mission. I rescued your paint, and you can rescue me by giving me something to keep busy."

"I don't want you to think I'm helpless. . . ."

"Are you going to rescue me, Sarah?" His eyes were full of mysteries she couldn't begin to comprehend. She looked into them for a long time, lost in the contemplation of his secrets. "Are you?" he added softly.

"Yes," she whispered.

"Then show me, Sarah." His smile was genuine

this time, free of ghosts. "I'll paint while you take care of Jenny."

"Come. It's my bedroom." His eyes got dark as she led the way. She didn't know why she had felt compelled to identify the room, except, of course, that her bed was in there, big as you please. She guessed he'd have figured it out anyway. "Blue on the walls, ivory on the trim," she added to cover her own turmoil. "I've always been partial to blue. It ma'... me think of being outside, surrounded by sky."

"I've always been partial to blue too." He was looking directly into her eyes when he said it, holding her attention with his powerful gaze until she could hardly breathe.

"Yes . . . well . . ." She forced herself to look away.

The paint buckets rattled as he bent over them. It was an ordinary sound that brought her back to reality.

"I'll come back to help you as soon as I feed and bathe Jenny and tuck her into bed. Routine is very important to her. I suppose it gives her a small sense of control in a world that's beyond her grasp."

"Take your time. I paint better than I mow lawns."

"I thought you were really good at that."

"You did?" He looked up from the paint, his eyes shining with pleasure. She had a hard time looking away.

"Indeed, I did. And so did Jenny. She loves running without weeds to impede her progress."

"I will do anything for Jenny," he said quietly.

"So will I."

His eyes drew her, caught her, held her. She couldn't look away. *Anything for Jenny*, he said. The words still hung in the air, sweet, reassuring. Sarah caught a stray curl and tucked it behind her ear. *Anything for Jenny . . . for Jenny . . . for Jenny.*

Jake was in her house because of his generosity toward her daughter. She would have to remember that.

She breathed deeply, then turned toward the door. Behind her, Jake rattled paint cans. He sounded all business. Well, that was exactly what she needed. Somebody who was all business, with no silly notions. Though how she would ever repay his many kindnesses was a mystery to her.

She tried to make quick work of Jenny's evening routine, but Jenny would have none of it. She was accustomed to a leisurely supper, a bubble bath with her rubber duck and two rubber whales, and then three bedtime stories. Sarah tried for two, but Jenny insisted.

"No! More. More."

Sarah sighed, impatient with her daughter for the first time in a long while. She wanted to say, "No. I have other things to do." But she didn't. How could she deny Jenny anything? And why was she impatient in the first place? All because Jake Townsend was in her bedroom with his compelling green eyes and his broad back that felt warm against her cheek, and his sweet, sad smile that made her want to cuddle him close.

Oh, Sarah Love, a fine kettle of fish you've gotten yourself into. Pining after a man you hardly know. But she knew his smile. She knew the sound of his voice. She knew the miracle of his touch.

Common sense told her to send him away . . . now, before things got too complicated, before Jenny became attached to him. *Jenny? What about yourself?*

She picked up a book and read Jenny's third story, but her mind was somewhere in her bedroom with a green-eyed man. How could she send him away? How could she bear to think of looking down the dusty road and never catching a glimpse of him? How could she endure a tea party in the yard he had mowed, knowing she might never see his face again?

Jenny had drifted asleep by the time Sarah finished the last story. She leaned down and tucked the sheet around her daughter, then kissed her softly on the cheek.

"Good night, my little special princess. Sweet dreams."

Sarah placed the book back on the shelf, then turned toward her bedroom. Jake was waiting.

Four

Jake's back was to the door, but he knew the minute Sarah entered the room. There was a sudden sense of electricity in the air as she charged the room with her presence. A shudder ran deeply through him, as if every fiber in his body were straining to be free.

He gripped the handle of the paintbrush harder than he had to and kept on painting. Blue, the color of Sarah's eyes.

He fancied he smelled her fragrance, but that was impossible, of course. A silly fantasy. The smell of fresh paint filled the room, too strong to allow perfume. Still, he dreamed the scent. Just as he dreamed being a hero. He was standing in Sarah's bedroom with his eyes wide open, dreaming that he was some noble character out of a novel, rescuing a beautiful woman in distress. And all along she was rescuing him, blackhearted thief that he was.

Her shoes tapped against the hardwood floors as she approached him. All his senses vibrated with her nearness.

"I see you covered the furniture." Her voice was soft and musical.

"Yes. I found sheets in the closet. I hope you don't mind." He didn't turn around. Her furniture consisted of an old dressing table with a cracked mirror, a rocking chair with a patchwork cushion, and the bed. The bed was somewhere behind him and Sarah, an old four-poster with one pillow, soft and dented looking. He had noticed. He imagined Sarah's hair spread bright upon that pillow. Depraved as he was, he even imagined himself touching her hair, stealing precious golden moments with her, pretending to be someone he was not.

"How could I mind, Jake? You've been absolutely wonderful to Jenny and me."

She brushed against his arm as she reached toward the paint can. Both of them pulled back, staring at each other. Her color was high and her eyes were a vivid blue, as if part of the morning sky had been spilled there.

An ache started deep in Jake's gut. Tears he had never shed gathered in his soul. All because of Sarah's blue eyes.

"Excuse me," she whispered.

"No problem."

"I thought I would help you finish this wall," she added.

"The work will go faster with two."

While they occupied themselves with paintbrushes Jake stole glances her way. Sometimes he caught her gaze upon him. In those shimmering moments, she would wet her lower lip with her tongue, then glance quickly away.

Jake wanted to taste her mouth, to feel her tongue seek his. Need rose in him, majestic and overpowering. He had to get out of her bedroom, out of her presence. And yet he couldn't. He had promised to paint.

"Jenny's sleeping."

"What?" He turned to her, disconnected to anything except his overwhelming need.

Sarah's eyes widened. She *knew*.

"I said, 'Jenny's sleeping.'"

"That's good."

The child was asleep and they were alone in the bedroom with passion scenting the air and Sarah's eyes so bright, they burned. Jake carefully laid the brush across the paint can and stepped closer to her.

Her hand tightened on her paintbrush, but she didn't move. He stepped closer, ever closer. Time stretched out, so that he seemed to be approaching her across a giant obstacle course.

He lifted one hand and carefully brushed back the curl that loved to caress her cheek. Her skin was soft, so very soft.

"Sarah," he whispered. With his hand still on her cheek, he lingered, caught in the heady passions that coursed through him and the knowledge that they were alone.

"Yes?"

"Sarah," he whispered once more, moving his hand over her cheek, exulting in the feel of her silky skin against his fingertips. In a moment of revelation he understood that mere passion would not be enough with Sarah. She was the kind of woman a man longed to possess.

She was so close, so sweet, so receptive. All he had to do was ease his arms around her, then bend down and cover her lips with his. He wondered if he would be able to taste their heart shape. Her warm breath fanned his cheek.

"Jake . . ." Was she asking him whether he meant to kiss her? Or was she giving him permission to do so?

He knew how precious her arms would feel around him. On the motorcycle with the evening wind in their hair, he had felt her caress. He edged closer. Sarah tipped her face upward.

Her eyes looked directly into his, and he saw blue for time without end, blue as the ocean under sunlight, blue as the pansies that bloomed beside his front door, blue as . . . death.

With a sound that was half moan, half curse, he backed away.

"Jake?" Sarah put her hand on his arm. "Is anything wrong?"

"Nothing." He picked up his paintbrush, then feeling guilty for his behavior, he offered explanation. "Forgive me, Sarah. For a moment I thought you were someone else."

"Oh." She looked crestfallen. He had only made matters worse.

His entire body was stiff as he turned back to his painting. Sarah's hand was still on his arm, scorching the skin.

"Is there anything I can do to help, Jake?"

"No . . . thank you."

"Sometimes you seem so tense, almost haunted." He jerked as if someone had socked him in the stomach. "Friendship works both ways, you know," Sarah added. She was patting his arm now, little butterfly taps that set his nerve endings a-tingle. "I don't have much chance for real adult relationships, but in my little shop, customers sometimes tell me their problems." She stepped closer and smiled directly into his face. "I'm a good listener, Jake."

"I'm sure you are, Sarah."

She held his gaze for a long time, as if she were trying to discover his secrets by looking into his eyes. He had heard they were the windows to the soul, but he hoped that wasn't true. If Sarah was seeing his soul, she was staring directly into torment.

"Forgive me for prying," she finally said, pulling her hand away.

"No." He caught her wrist, forcing her to look at him. Her eyes grew wide and startled. Letting go, he silently cursed himself for being a fool. "It's not you, Sarah; it's me. I'm a private man." *A lonely man.*

"I understand." She smiled. "Not everybody is like me." She picked up her own paintbrush and, squaring her shoulders, set to work.

For a while there was no sound in the room except the swish of paintbrushes against the wall and the rise and fall of their breathing. Then Sarah broke the silence.

"Remember the first day we met . . . the day you brought a yellow rose to Jenny in the backyard?" Without waiting for a reply, she hurried on. "I confided in you, all in a rush. I don't usually do that with strangers, Jake. It's just that there is something so good in you, so caring, so decent. . . ."

Her praise was balm to his soul. He could have listened to it forever.

"Don't paint me a saint, Sarah."

"Can I paint you a good friend?" She turned suddenly, smiling. A small glob of blue paint flew off her brush and landed on the tip of his nose.

"Oh dear," she said, covering her mouth to hold back the laughter. "I'm so sorry."

"Did you just paint my nose?" He was so relieved with a change of topic, he had a hard time pretending outrage.

"I'm afraid I did." One giggle escaped her, then another, until Sarah was caught in a full-blown fit of mirth.

"Lady, when you asked if you could paint me a friend I didn't think you meant it literally."

"I'm a very literal woman." She was laughing so hard, she could hardly talk. She set her paintbrush down and wiped tears from her eyes. "Blue happens to be your color."

"It is, is it?" Jake touched his nose and his finger came away blue. Caught in the joy of the moment, he became playful. "I wonder what your color is?" With one swipe he painted a blue streak on her nose. "Now we match."

"Not quite." Sarah bent over the can and came back with blue fingers. Jake knew what was coming, but he didn't try to dodge. In fact, he bent down so she could reach him.

Laughing, she put both hands on his cheeks. "Let's see how you look with a blue nose *and* blue cheeks."

First Jake felt the paint, sticky and wet. Both of them were laughing. Then Sarah stood on tiptoe and he leaned down. Her hands stilled, and awareness sparked in her eyes. Their laughter died.

Jake didn't take time to think, to reason. He acted on instinct. Sarah's mouth was warm under his, warm and sweet and inviting. He could taste the heart shape, just as he had imagined. And it was wonderful.

He drew her close with one arm, never taking his lips from hers. She sighed, and it was the sweetest sound Jake had ever heard. A woman sighing for him. A sweet brave woman with the heart of a saint and the spirit of a soldier.

Tender feelings pushed up from the darkness of his heart, and a joy that had long lain dormant tried to be reborn. If Jake had believed in second chances, he would have thought Sarah was his. But he knew better. There was no such thing as a second chance.

What had been done couldn't be undone, not even with the magic balm of Sarah's kiss.

There was no redemption for him, but there was solace. And he took it, there in Sarah's arms, in her bedroom with the scent of fresh paint around them. *Just this moment*, he told himself, holding on to Sarah. A selfish beast reared its ugly head in him and demanded more.

He fitted her to his body, gloating at how perfect they were together, as if heaven had fashioned her just for him. Heaven . . . or hell. The kiss became sweet torment. Jake wanted more. His body demanded more.

Sarah sighed once again, melting into him. He had to let her go. Already he had stolen too much from her. He couldn't risk more; he couldn't consign them both to hell.

Letting go was sweet torture, but better sweet torture than eternal agony. He released her and stepped back. She caught the windowsill for balance. Her lips were puffy where he had kissed them. She looked disheveled and delicious . . . and stunned.

"Forgive me, Sarah. I had no right to do that." It was a first for him, apologizing for kissing a woman.

"Oh." She touched her lips and studied him with wise eyes.

"I didn't mean to take advantage of you." He picked up his paintbrush.

"No . . . no. You didn't." She picked up her own paintbrush. "What I mean is . . . I'm a grown woman, Jake."

"You're a wonderful woman with great responsibilities." His hand was tight on the paintbrush as he made vicious swipes at the wall. The damned thing seemed to have grown bigger. "I have no intention of using you for my own selfish needs. I hope you understand."

"I do." Her voice was small. He dared not look at her.

They busied themselves with painting, never taking their eyes off the wall. The silence stretched and stretched until it grew uncomfortable.

"Jake?"

Finally he looked at her. She was as serenely beautiful as ever, even with the blue paint on her nose. He felt the paint drying on his own face. He had forgotten the damned stuff.

"I don't want you to let this change things," she said, her cheeks rosy. "I mean . . ." She wet her lips with her tongue. Jake wanted to feel it on his own lips. He got a grip on his paintbrush and his passions. ". . . the kiss . . ." Her voice trailed off again.

"It's all right, Sarah." He dared not touch her, even to pat her hand. "Nothing has changed." He added lying to his list of sins.

"What I meant to say was, when Jenny forms a friendship, she doesn't understand if it's broken." Sarah held the paintbrush upright with both hands, almost as if she were praying. "I don't want to be the cause of driving away a friend of Jenny's."

"Sarah, I promise you that I will always be Jenny's friend." She still looked troubled. "No matter what," he added. That seemed to settle matters in Sarah's mind.

"Thank you," she said, smiling at him. "That's done, then. We'll think no more about it."

Sarah with her beautiful soul had neatly extricated him from a dangerous situation. With a few brave words she had put the kiss and all the feelings it had inspired into a box and nailed the lid shut. Jake was spared the need to run. Not only had Sarah given him permission, she had almost begged him to stick around. He would. But in the future he would be more careful. He would look but not touch.

He smiled at Sarah, loving the radiance that shone in her face. Even looking brought joy. He guessed he was entitled to that much . . . occasionally. If he didn't get used to it. If he didn't start thinking he couldn't live without it.

They worked until the room was complete. If Sarah was suffering any pangs of fear or remorse for having kissed him, she gave no outward sign.

"To show my appreciation," Sarah said as they scrubbed paintbrushes, "I'll fry chicken tomorrow for a picnic."

Jake hesitated. It was late. Tomorrow was only a few hours away. Could he recover sufficiently from the night's encounter? Could he put it far enough behind him so he wasn't tempted to do it again?

"Of course, if you're busy, I'll certainly understand." She fussed with her hair. "It's just . . . I thought a picnic might be nice . . . Jenny loves them so."

He had hurt her. He could see the feeling of being rejected in her eyes. He didn't ever want to hurt Sarah Love.

"I'll be here." He made his tone jovial. "You provide the fried chicken, and I'll provide the horse."

"The horse?"

"Yes. At my place. I have horses."

"Jenny will love that." Sarah clapped her hands with delight.

Will you love it too? Will you love sitting in front of me with your warm back pressed against my chest?

Jake put such thoughts from his mind. Surely there was enough humanity left in him to be a friend.

"Good," he said. "I'll pick you up around eleven."

They bade each other a polite good night. He was home before he remembered the blue paint on his face. He was solemn as he studied the stripes in the bathroom mirror. Sarah had left her mark on him.

Sarah couldn't sleep in her bedroom because of the fresh paint smells. She dragged an old sleeping bag out of the closet and made her bed in the hall. Then she blamed the hard floor for ruining her sleep. But she knew that wasn't so. Deep down she knew Jake was the reason she wasn't sleeping. He had kissed her, and she had loved it.

Wonder and terror mixed together in her mind until she could hardly tell one from the other. What if she fell in love? What if, miracle of miracles, Jake fell in love with her? What if they got married? He was a vital, powerful man. He would want children. What if Sarah's time were divided with another child? What if the other child were special?

Sarah groaned and covered her head with the sheet.

"Stop it," she said aloud. "Stop this nonsense right now."

She supposed she was the silliest woman alive, worrying about having children with a man who had sworn never to kiss her again. Well, he hadn't said that, exactly. But he had apologized profusely. Why? Because he hadn't liked the kiss? He had seemed to like it.

She was being foolish again. What did it matter whether Jake Townsend had enjoyed the kiss? There would never be love, never be marriage, never be another child.

"Sarah Love, you're turning into a dreamer."

She tried to shut Jake out by closing her eyes.

Nothing has changed, he had said. Hadn't he felt the heavens move? Hadn't he felt the sky tip its load of stars into his heart?

Sarah groaned, twisting herself and the sheets into a knot beside the sleeping bag. It would be wise to get at least a few hours' sleep. She had chicken to fry tomorrow. And she had Jenny.

At precisely eleven o'clock the next morning Jake was standing on Sarah's front porch, ringing her doorbell. Sarah and Jenny came to the door almost before the bell had finished ringing. They were scrubbed and shining, and the sight of them fairly took his breath away.

"Hello." Sarah's smile was shy. He guessed memories of the previous night were as fresh to her as they were to him. He could still taste her lips.

"Good morning," he said, equally restrained.

Jenny was not so restrained. " 'ake!" she screamed, then threw her arms around his legs.

"Hi, Jenny." He bent to pick Jenny up. "The nicest thing about children," he said, holding her in his arms, "is getting hugged around the knees."

"She's quite affectionate. I hope you don't mind."

"Mind?" With Jenny's little arms around him he felt whole once more, as if his past had never happened. "I love it. A hug from Jenny is just what I need today." *And every day. A hug to remember Bonnie by. A hug without the responsibility.* He felt selfish, but not enough to turn and walk away. Sarah and Jenny needed a friend. Surely he could allow himself a little emotion for a few hours each day. After six years of disuse, his cold heart could use the exercise.

"Are you ready?" he asked Sarah.

"Let me get the picnic basket."

She disappeared in the direction of the kitchen. While she was gone, Jenny patted Jake's face all over.

"Nice man. Nice 'ake."

"Sometimes you make me believe that, Jenny. Sometimes, when I lie awake in my bed, remembering all the ways I failed Bonnie, I think of you and your mother, and somehow, the ghosts go away." He pressed his lips to Jenny's soft hair. "Jenny, sweet little Jenny. I'm glad you don't understand what I'm saying. I'm glad you think of me as nice."

Jake was aware of being watched. He looked up to see Sarah standing just inside the screen door, the picnic basket in her hand and a smile on her face. He didn't know if she had been there long enough to hear. He hoped not. He had already shown too much of himself to Sarah.

"Ready?" he said.

"Ready."

They loaded everything into his car and started across town to his house. The Townsend Mansion, everybody in Florence called it. To Jake it was just home. It was a classic structure of mortar and brick that had probably witnessed more tragedy than any other house in town.

"It's beautiful," Sarah said as they got out of the car.

Jenny ran ahead of them and began plucking the heads off the pansies that bordered his sidewalk.

"Pretty. Pretty."

"Oh, Jenny. No." Sarah started after her daughter.

"Let her." Jake put his hand on her arm. "They're just flowers."

"She loves them. I plan to make a flower bed at home." Sarah fussed at her hair. The sun got caught in her eyes. So blue. Jake couldn't look away. Jenny became a faraway voice chanting, "Pretty, pretty."

Self-conscious, Sarah talked in a breathless rush, her voice spilling over his senses like a summer waterfall. He was refreshed, enchanted. And he wanted to kiss her all over again.

"There are so many things I want to do with our new house," she said. "Get a porch swing, for one. I love a porch swing. They're so pleasant in the summer. And Jenny loves to swing." Her gaze held his, and the summer sun held them both in a warm sweet embrace.

"Hmmm," he said, not capable of more.

"Of course, I guess it's not practical to be thinking of porch swings and flower beds when there are so many other things my house needs . . . new porch steps, for starters." She lifted her bright hair again, and Jake remembered touching it. So soft. Her hair was so soft.

"Oh dear, just listen to me, going on like this. I'll bet Jenny has beheaded all your flowers by now."

Still, she didn't turn away. Both of them were bewitched by the sun, the summer air, the stolen moment.

For a little while Jake allowed himself the luxury of feeling, of dreaming. Tenderness warmed his heart and dreams tugged at his mind. He pictured Sarah and Jenny in his home, belonging to him. He imagined himself being noble and strong and kind and loving. But most of all, he imagined himself as their protector, always keeping them from harm.

"Mine," Jenny demanded, tugging at Jake's pant legs. She was holding an armful of bedraggled pansies, roots and all. Dirt covered her face and hands, but she was smiling and happy.

Jake knelt beside her. "Yes, Jenny. They are yours." He took her grimy little hand. "I have something else you'll like. Do you want to go and see?"

"See?"

He glanced at Sarah. "She's asking you what do you want her to see?"

"It's a surprise, Jenny. Do you want to see a surprise?"

Jenny furrowed her brow and studied him long and hard before she gave her answer. Finally she smiled. "Yes."

They started across his well-kept lawn together. Jake glanced over his shoulder. Sarah stood beside the walk, watching them.

"Are you coming, Sarah?"

"Yes." She smiled. "Oh, yes. I wouldn't miss this for anything in the world."

"Her name is Martha Lynn," Jake explained when they reached the kennels. The golden retriever looked up at the sound of her name.

"Dog. Big dog." Jenny pressed her face against the fence. "Big dog."

"Do you like her, Jenny?"

"Yes, yes, yes," she chanted, clapping her hands.

"Someday I'm going to get her a little dog at the animal shelter. She loves animals."

"Animals love her," Jake said. "Look at that."

Martha Lynn had walked to the fence and was busy licking Jenny's hand. Jenny giggled.

Jake and Sarah stepped back to watch the happy twosome, dog and child, made to be together. Jenny glanced up at Jake, smiling, but all he saw were her blue eyes.

Can I have a 'prise, Daddy? Can I? Can I?

Of course you can, sweetheart. Daddy's little girl can have anything she wants.

Anything, Daddy?

Anything, Bonnie. The moon, the sun, the stars. You name it.

*I want a puppy, and I want her name to be
Martha Lynn.*

Jake struggled to push the ghosts to the back of
his mind, but he didn't succeed until Jenny turned
back to the dog.

"How would you feel about getting Jenny a dog
now?"

"I can't afford—we're just getting settled in."

"A golden retriever puppy complete with a lifetime
guarantee of dog food and vet visits."

"Martha Lynn has puppies?"

"She does."

"And you're offering to give Jenny an expensive
pedigreed dog. . . . She does have a pedigree, I as-
sume?"

"Yes."

"Complete with dog food and paid-up vet bills."

"Yes."

Sarah studied him a long time. "Why?" she finally
asked.

He could have lied. He could have told Sarah he just
wanted to give Jenny a dog, that he wanted Martha
Lynn's puppies to have a good home. But he couldn't
lie, not to Sarah.

"Because Jenny reminds me of someone else."

Sarah didn't ask who, but stood still, waiting.
Bonnie came to his mind, alive and laughing as if it
had been only yesterday that she'd stood beside the
kennels with her new puppy. Jake's throat closed,
and he couldn't say any more.

Sarah touched his arm gently. "I can see you must
have loved that special someone very much."

Jake nodded, still too full of memories to speak.

"You are much too generous, but how can I say
no?" Sarah squeezed his arm. "Thank you, Jake.
Jenny will thank you, too, in her way."

He looked at his arm where Sarah's hand rested. It was a precious touch, for there was no artfulness in Sarah, no pretense. He covered her hand with his.

"Sarah, you're very sweet."

"Oh." She drew the sound out, so that her mouth stayed shaped for the longest while. Jake struggled with the temptation to lean down and kiss her. They held each other with their eyes until Sarah finally pulled her hand away. Then she reached up and tucked in the curl that always curved onto her cheek.

"No one has ever called me sweet before."

"They should have, because you are."

They got caught up in looking at each other once more. Finally Sarah sighed, then smiled.

"Don't paint me too sweet, Jake."

"I can't. I don't have any blue paint."

They both laughed. Jenny turned to see what was going on. Seeing nothing out of the ordinary, she grabbed both of them by the pant legs and pulled.

"Big dog, big dog," she said. Then she gave a great imitation of Martha Lynn's tongue hanging out.

"You're a little mimic." Sarah bent over her daughter and scooped her up. "Shall I tell her now, Jake?"

"Yes."

"Jenny, Jake is giving you a puppy of your very own."

"Big dog?"

"No, it will be a little dog, a very little dog, and you'll have to be careful with it so it will grow up to be a big dog."

"Me?"

"Yes, Jenny. A little dog just for you."

Jenny still wasn't convinced. She furrowed her brow and looked first at her mother then at Jake.

"Hug dog?" She wrapped her arms around herself to demonstrate.

"Yes, my precious. You can hug him."

"I'll get one for her." Jake went into the kennel and selected a fat female from the litter, all the time thinking about Jenny. In two words she had communicated a universal need of all living creatures—to be loved. Sometimes even he fit into that category, for there he was, attending a picnic, basking in Jenny's love and Sarah's admiration. He could take what he wanted and, at the end of the day, walk away. That was the good part about being a friend to Jenny and Sarah. He could walk away. No commitments, no involvement, but most of all, no heartbreak, no pain that burned the mind and seared the soul.

He guessed that made him selfish. Cold, heartless, careless, selfish. He was setting quite a track record.

That kind of thinking was sure to put a pall on a good day. With an effort he cleared his mind and left the kennel. Then he gave the puppy to Jenny and stood back to watch. It was almost like seeing Bonnie all over again. After her initial squeal of delight, Jenny picked up her puppy, then laid her head against the soft fur and began to croon.

Until that moment he didn't know it was possible to be sad and happy at the same time.

"Thank you," Sarah said.

"Thank *you*, Sarah."

She understood. Without asking why, she seemed to know that she had given as much as she had received. Standing on tiptoe, she kissed Jake's cheek. He felt as if he were free-falling from a plane. Somewhere below him was the ground, but he wasn't sure exactly where he would land, or in what condition. He decided to pull the rip cord before it was too late.

"If I'm not mistaken, there's some fried chicken in that basket we left in the car. And I'm starved."

"Good. I cooked enough for a big man like you."

"I'll make certain that all your work is not in vain, Sarah."

She reached for his hand in another of her totally artless gestures. Going down the path with Sarah laughing and chatting and Jenny following along with her new puppy, Jake knew contentment. He tightened his hold on Sarah's hand, wishing the day could last forever.

Five

They spread the picnic lunch beside a lake. Jenny was too excited about her puppy to eat more than a bite, but Jake didn't let any chicken go to waste. Grinning like a schoolboy, he ate piece after piece.

"This is delicious." Bits of crust decorated his mouth. His uninhibited enthusiasm reminded Sarah of Jenny.

"Have another piece." She passed him another leg and watched as he took a big bite.

"Mmm. Magnificent." His eyes shone with delight.

Sarah couldn't remember a time she had been happier or more content. Jake was showing a side of himself she had never seen, a playful man, capable of childlike wonder and joy in the simple things of life.

She leaned against the trunk of the oak tree and watched Jake. In the corner of her vision she saw Jenny, romping with her puppy.

"You look happy, Sarah."

"Summertime does that to me." *And you*.

"I'm glad you came." He waved a bone at her, laughing. "And not just for the chicken."

She waited for him to elaborate, not realizing she was holding her breath until he started speaking again.

"Once this estate was filled with laughter. You and Jenny brought the laughter back." He gazed across the lake, seeing things she couldn't see. When he turned back, the playful man had disappeared and a haunted man looked at her. "All that was a very long time ago."

"What was a long time ago, Jake?"

For a moment he looked as if he might tell her, and then he had another of his mercurial mood changes.

"Did I promise you a horse?" The laughter was back in his eyes.

"Indeed, you did."

"Never let it be said I'm not a man of my word." He reached for her hand and pulled her up. "Come. Let's find the horse."

They collected Jenny and, after promising her a horseback ride, convinced her to put her new puppy in the kennels.

Jake's stables were filled with fine horses. He selected his most gentle one for the ride.

"This one is called Slowpoke." It was a beautiful black mare.

"She looks capable of running the Kentucky Derby to me."

"Are you afraid of horses, Sarah?"

"Not if I have somebody big and strong to hold on to."

"A hero?"

There was a wistful quality to his voice. Sarah knew she was seeing an important truth about Jake Townsend. He longed to be a hero.

"Yes, Jake. A hero." She put her hand on his arm. "And you will be perfect."

"You almost make me believe that."

The haunted look was in his eyes again. Impulsively Sarah threw her arms around him, hugging tightly. Mingled scents of grass and hay and the fresh outdoors clung to his shirt. He smelled masculine . . . and wonderful. Sarah got confused. Was she hugging Jake for herself or for him? When she had thrown her arms around him, her intention had been to comfort. Now she wasn't sure what her intentions were.

He hugged back, and for a moment they stood with her head on his chest and his arms circling her waist and their hearts thumping in rhythm as if they had been designed by angels to do so.

"Believe it, Jake. Believe it," she whispered.

"Sarah . . ." He tangled his hands in her hair and gently eased her head back so he could see her face. His eyes were dark in the semi-gloom of the stable, the intense green of hardwood trees deep in a forest, dark and mysterious and compelling. His warm breath stirred the hair at her temples, and she thought he was going to kiss her. *Please*, she said silently, but she didn't know whether she was saying please do or please don't.

She longed to feel the heavens sprinkle stars on her soul, and yet she knew she could not, *must* not encourage Jake to intimacy. She had enough in her life to deal with. How could she possibly handle more?

"Now about that horse," she said, breaking the spell that held them captive.

Jake stepped back, and she thought she saw relief on his face. That was all well and good, she decided as he set about saddling the horse. She should be relieved too. Only she wasn't. She was forlorn and puzzled and maybe a little disappointed. Truth to tell, she was a *lot* disappointed.

Oh, she was becoming a selfish woman. Here Jake was, giving her a glorious day, and she wanted more. Never mind that she should be thinking of Jenny. She was going to have to do something about herself. And soon. Before she got into real trouble.

She was still brooding on her sins when Jake trotted the horse out and suggested they all saddle up.

"All of us?" she asked.

"That's the only way I can keep you safe."

And so they all ended up on the horse, with Jenny in Jake's lap and Sarah sitting behind, circling her arms around him once more. *Lord, are you playing jokes today? Sending more temptation than I can bear?*

She clung to Jake's back and tried not to feel buttery soft and warm inside, tried not to dream of things that could never be.

"I can bear it. I have to," she said aloud. Fortunately, the wind took her voice away and Jake never heard.

Jake was an expert horseman. Sarah decided that he was an expert at everything. Clinging to his back, with the rhythm of the horse under her and the wind caressing her face, she wondered if he would be an expert at lovemaking. What would Jake say if he knew? He would probably run like the devil. Land sakes, she was getting depraved since she'd moved from Birmingham. Maybe it was something in the Florence air.

"That's enough for today," Jake said. "Jenny is all tuckered out."

It seemed the ride had just begun, and now it was over. Jake helped Sarah off the horse. When she felt his arms around her, she wanted to slide toward his chest and just keep on going until the two of them were in a tangled heap on the ground. Panting. She actually wanted to be panting.

"I guess I'm tired too."

"In that case, I'd better take both of you home."

Now she had done it. She didn't want to go home. Home was a place without Jake. Nevertheless, she walked along beside him back to the stables as he held Jenny in his arms and led the horse.

By the time he turned the horse over to a groom, Jenny's head was nodding on Jake's shoulder. Sarah would never forget the look on his face as long as she lived. She saw disbelief, then wonder, then joy.

He started singing, so softly at first, she thought she had imagined the song. Then his voice got stronger, and it was a beautiful baritone. He was singing a lullaby. Jenny snuggled close and was soon fast asleep.

After they got into the car, he laid Jenny gently on Sarah's lap, careful not to wake her. Still mindful of his sleeping cargo, he didn't talk going home. That was just as well. Sarah couldn't think of a thing that would do to say out loud.

She was thinking plenty of other things. *Where will you go after you take us home? Is there a beautiful woman waiting for you? One without a child?*

She was ashamed of herself. Almost wishing to be carefree when she had the most precious gift of all—Jenny.

When they got to her house, Jake insisted on carrying Jenny inside.

"She's getting almost too big for you to carry," he said.

Her heart seemed to grow as she watched Jake

carry her daughter up the steps, careful of the rickety board. She opened the door for him, and he carried Jenny inside, all the way to her little bed.

Sarah stood beside the door and watched him tuck Jenny in. *He's done it before.* The thought crystallized so suddenly that Sarah was caught off guard. What a silly thing to be thinking. Just because Jake looked so natural . . . He would be a wonderful father. If only . . .

"Sarah . . ."

"Yes?"

"Thank you for a wonderful day."

"You're the one who deserves the thanks."

He came to her in the doorway, and they stood together, crowded, his legs brushing against hers. She wished she could think of a clever ploy to keep him that way. It was a foolish notion, of course. She couldn't keep Jake standing in a doorway forever.

"Tell Jenny good-bye for me when she wakes up from her nap."

"I will."

He still stood there with his leg touching hers. It was wonderful.

"Well . . . I should be going."

"I suppose. . . ."

"Good-bye, Sarah."

"Good-bye." She stood in the doorway of Jenny's bedroom and watched him walk down the hall. He let himself out the front door, and then he was gone.

Sarah felt glued to the spot. She smoothed her blouse and fussed with her hair. Jake was gone and so was the warm glow inside her. When he had said he had to be going, why hadn't she suggested he stay for a glass of lemonade? She might even have served cookies.

What would have been the point? She went into

the kitchen and had lemonade and cookies all by herself.

Sarah pressed the memory of the picnic between the pages of her mind like a flower. Every day she took the memory out and looked at it, and each time she did, she found it fresh and beautiful. Jake, with crusts from the fried chicken on his mouth and merriment dancing in his eyes. Jake, wrapping his arms around her as he helped her onto the horse, holding her in his solid embrace. Jake, cradling Jenny's bright head against his shoulder, singing to her until she fell asleep.

It had been a day made in paradise. Sarah sighed and turned back to her sewing. She had dolls to make. Useless dreaming didn't pay the bills.

She hadn't seen Jake in three days, and chances were she wouldn't see him again for a long time. After all, he was a busy man. He was also unattached and probably had a line of females a mile long waiting for his attentions. He had vowed friendship, but that didn't mean he would spend every waking minute with her and Jenny. That didn't even necessarily mean he would ever see them again. After all, Bobby Wayne had declared love till death do us part, and look what had happened to him.

"Stop it, Sarah Love," she whispered to herself. If she kept up with that line of thinking, she was going to get absolutely maudlin.

Sarah glanced at her daughter before she put the finishing touch on the doll pinafore she was making. Jenny was sitting on the floor teaching her puppy how to color.

"Red, 'ake. Red," she insisted, holding the crayon under his nose. She had named her puppy Jake, never mind that it was female. She selected another crayon and showed it to the puppy. "Yellow, 'ake. Yellow."

Jenny didn't know half the things other four-year-olds did, but she did know colors. Sarah supposed it was the artist in her.

Sarah put the finished pinafore on a doll, then set the doll on the shelf.

"Snack time, Jenny."

" 'ake too?"

"Yes. Jake too."

Sarah went through her afternoon routine, snack then a game with Jenny, then nap time. When Jenny was sleeping, she went back into her shop. It wasn't a shop, really. It was a large sunny room on the west side of the house, with a picture window that faced the road and its own entrance. Sarah had hung her sign the day before—THE DOLLHOUSE.

Before she sat down to her sewing, she went to the window and looked out. No sign of customers. She shaded her eyes and squinted into the afternoon sun. No sign of Jake. Not even a puff of dust on the road.

How silly of her to be looking. She had been watching out the window for three days, and it hadn't done a bit of good. Jake was not coming.

She sighed and went back to her sewing.

"Are you going to dictate a letter, or do you plan to stare out the window all afternoon?"

Jake turned from the window. Gwendolyn had a steno pad in her hands and a look of mutiny on her face. He knew he was in for a lecture.

"All right, Gwendolyn. What's on your mind?"

"What's on *your* mind? You've been mully-grubbing around here for three days."

"I have a lot to think about."

"Like what?"

"That's a nosy question."

"I'm a nosy woman." She glared at him. "Well?"

"Where do you want me to start, Gwendolyn?"

"How about starting by telling me how come you never showed up at the art gallery Saturday night. You never miss an opening."

"I was painting."

"Since when did you become an artist."

"I was painting a room."

"Painting a room? Since when can't the richest man in town afford a painter?"

He decided to make her work hard for her information. Both of them had more fun that way. He ignored her question.

"Let's see . . . you mowed a yard, even drove the lawn mower through the city streets after dark. Could have gotten yourself killed." She gave him an arch smile. "Didn't you figure half the town would see you and report directly to me?"

"What other reports have you heard?"

"Why, Jake. You do me an injustice. Do you think I'd stoop to petty gossip? If I want to find out something about you, all I have to do is ask."

"How do you know I'll tell you the truth?"

"Hell, Jake. I'm your mother and your father confessor and your favorite maiden aunt all rolled into one. Not to mention your good friend and the best executive assistant you'll ever find this side of heaven."

"It's a good thing I wasn't looking for modesty when I hired you."

Gwendolyn laid her steno pad aside and squinted at him. "So, tell me. Does all this yard mowing and house painting have anything to do with that yellow rose and certain people who live in an old house at the edge of town?"

"Yes."

"Be careful, Jake."

She was echoing what he had been telling himself for the last three days. His Good Samaritan act was getting out of control.

"I hear she's pretty," Gwendolyn added.

"Who?"

"The mother, Sarah Love."

"She is."

"And she has a child . . . about the age Bonnie was."

"Yes." He couldn't face Gwendolyn now. She was too wise. He swiveled his chair and gazed out the window.

"You can't bring her back, Jake." He kept staring out the window. "Did you hear me, Jake? Don't try to use this child as a substitute. You'll get hurt."

"They are the ones who would be hurt, Gwendolyn." He faced her once more. "I would never do that to them."

They studied each other like two wise old lions in the same arena.

"Just so you know what you're doing."

"I do." He didn't know whether he was lying. He sincerely hoped not. He stood up, full of resolve and purpose. "Look, Gwendolyn. Forget the letter. Take the afternoon off."

"Why?"

"Don't question your good fortune. Just go."

After Gwendolyn left, he picked up the phone and placed his order.

"Deliver it in half an hour," he instructed. That gave him exactly fifteen minutes at Sarah's before the delivery truck arrived, five if he stopped at the hardware store for hammer and nails.

He decided to stop. Sarah's porch steps needed repairing. It would be a good way to say good-bye.

Jake saw the sign in Sarah's yard—THE DOLLHOUSE. She had opened her shop. That was good. It meant she would soon have other friends in Florence. With her personality, she would have so many friends in two weeks, she wouldn't even know he was gone, let alone miss him.

Darkness settled around his heart. He willed it to go away. Dammit, he was doing the right thing, the best thing for everybody. Emotions had no place in his decision.

He went around the side of her house to the shop entrance, intent on his errand. He would do one last repair job—the porch steps. But before he did, he would explain to Sarah why a friendship between them was impossible. Breaking his promise now would be easier than ruining their lives later.

When he was even with the picture window, he heard the music, a slow tune, sung the way blues should be sung. Memories paralyzed him.

Do you like blues? The woman had blue eyes and a friendly smile.

I like the music, not the mood.

Then I'll make certain you never suffer the mood. Hi, I'm Michelle. She'd offered her hand . . . and more.

He was young and full of red wine and hot blood. He took everything she'd had to offer. That fatal decision had altered the course of his life. In one careless night he'd fathered a child and set himself and Michelle on the path to destruction.

Jake brushed his hand across his eyes, dispelling the memories, ridding himself of ghosts. Music poured from the Dollhouse. He glanced through the window. Sarah was dancing slowly, around and around, head tilted so she could gaze up at her dance partner. The sun gilded her hair, kissed her skin, brightened her eyes.

Jake was enchanted. He couldn't take his eyes off her. To be holding her in his arms, revolving slowly around the room, blues music defining their steps, their mood—that would be heaven. He closed his eyes, dreaming.

Sarah. Sarah. She was like music in his mind, a remembered melody too sweet to forget.

She had a partner. He opened his eyes quickly and looked at Sarah's dance partner. It was a mop. Jake felt relieved and saddened at the same time, relieved that Sarah wasn't dancing with someone else, and sad that she had to dance with a mop.

The music played on and Sarah danced. He watched awhile longer, stealing precious glimpses of a brave and wonderful woman with blue eyes. Always blue eyes.

Jake groaned. Time to get moving. He wasn't about to destroy Sarah and Jenny the way he had destroyed Michelle and Bonnie.

He walked quickly around the side of the house and pushed open the shop door. Sarah whirled toward him.

"Oh." She pressed the mop to her chest. Color stained her cheeks.

"Sorry I startled you."

"I didn't expect to see you." She laid the mop across a chair and fussed with her hair. "I must look a mess."

"You're lovely."

The music swirled around them. Sarah's blue eyes trapped him. Forces beyond his control pulled at him. The blue eyes beckoned.

He crossed the room until he was so close, he could smell her perfume, feel her skirt brushing against his leg. Her eyes softened. He put a hand on her cheek.

"Hello, Sarah." The good-byes could wait.

"Hello." Her smile was shy. Her eyes bewitched him.

Sultry music whispered siren songs in his ear. His hand trembled on Sarah's cheek. He wanted to wrap himself around her until they merged, until he couldn't tell where he left off and she began. He wanted to lose his darkness in her sunlight and be cleansed. He wanted to obliterate his past with this blue-eyed woman who bravely walked sideways under her burdens.

How could he tell her good-bye? It would be cruel.

He trailed his fingers down her cheek. Then, unable to resist, he traced the outline of her mouth, memorizing its heart shape.

"I have a surprise for you," he said, removing his hand and backing away. He couldn't say good-bye, but he could control his passions. He had destroyed once; he would never do it again.

"For me?"

"Yes. Just for you."

Tears brightened her eyes, and she brushed at them with the back of her hand.

"I didn't mean to make you cry."

"I'm not . . . it's just that . . ." She blinked the last of her tears away and gave him a steadfast look. "The puppy was a different matter; it was for Jenny. But I can't accept gifts for myself."

"Why not?"

"I have nothing to give in return."

"You have everything to give in return, Sarah—your smile, your warmth, you kindness."

"It doesn't seem enough. You are too generous."

"Indulge me, Sarah. I don't mean to *buy* you, nor to make you feel obligated to me in any way. But I do want you to accept my gifts." His smile was rueful. "I'm more than able to afford them."

"I'm not used to receiving gifts." She gave him a sweet, shy smile. "Especially from heroes."

Why had he ever thought he could tell this woman good-bye? She was pure and innocent and warm and beautiful. She was the only good thing in his life. If he let her go, he would lose the part of himself that made him believe he might be human.

"I'm a selfish hero, Sarah."

"No."

"Yes. I give for my own pleasure."

"Oh, Jake." She came to him and circled her arms around his waist. Then she pressed her cheek against his chest. The need to possess her was so great, he trembled. "You have no idea, do you?" she whispered.

He tensed. His wife's words echoed from the past.

You have no idea, do you, Jake? No idea why I hate you so?

I'm certain you'll tell me.

Damned right, I'll tell you. Do you know what it's like to be married to someone who doesn't love you?

Yes. It was never love between us, Michelle. Only necessity.

Bonnie. It's always Bonnie with you.

Leave Bonnie out of this.

She's always there, between us. A reminder that you had to marry me. Well, you can have her. I'm tired of being viewed as a necessary evil. You can take your precious daughter and go straight to hell, where you belong. And I hope you burn forever knowing how much I despise you.

Sarah pressed her cheek against his heart. "I want you to know, Jake . . ."

"Don't . . ."

". . . just how wonderful I think you are."

He drew a ragged breath. If she knew the truth about him, she wouldn't be saying that. But he would never tell her, never let her know what he had done, just as he would never let her know that her simple hugs drove him crazy.

Her arms around his waist melted him. Her head against his chest set him aflame. Her sweet summer fragrance set off erotic fantasies that haunted him day and night.

When had a simple friendship gotten so out of control? How had he managed to steer clear of disaster for six years and then fall into the first tender trap he came to?

"You're going to give me a big head," he said, taking her by the arms and gently setting her aside.

"It's true. You're wonderful. I don't think you know that about yourself."

"Neither does anybody else. It's the town's best-kept secret."

"Then I'll make it my duty to inform them."

"No one has ever fought dragons for me." He smiled, hoping she would take his statement as a joke.

She smiled back. Letting him think she had.

"And no one has ever brought me a surprise. What is it?"

"It's no surprise if I tell." Jake heard the delivery truck outside, right on schedule. "Close your eyes, and don't open them until I tell you."

He took her hand and led her outside. She held on

tight, trusting and innocent. Jake felt as tall and noble as the Washington Monument.

"Keep your eyes closed, Sarah," he said. Then to the deliverymen: "Put it on the front porch . . . yes, that's right . . . there. That's perfect. Go ahead and install it."

"Install what? I'm dying of curiosity."

"You feel perfectly healthy to me." He squeezed her hand. Feeling lighthearted and playful, he ran his hands tenderly across her cheeks, down her neck, and down her arms, till he was holding her hands again. "Hmmm, very healthy. Except . . . what is that? A callus?"

"From sewing. I never can find my thimble."

"Are you forgetful, Sarah?"

"No, I never forget. . . ." Her eyelids fluttered.

"Keep your eyes closed, please."

"I forgot." She squeezed her eyes shut, then explained about the thimble. "Jenny loves to hide my thimble. She always hides it in the same place, the potted plant beside the door, but I pretend I don't know. It thrills her to think she's outfoxed me."

Dear Sarah. Always making the people around her feel good. She was a natural caretaker. She could be hurt so easily.

Jake looked at the color staining her cheeks. It was time to let her go—past time. He released her as the deliverymen passed by, on the way to their truck.

"The surprise is ready, Sarah. Open your eyes."

She opened them slowly, first one and then the other. Then she pressed her hands over her heart, her mouth open in wonder.

"Well?"

"Oh, Jake. A *swing*." She ran up the steps, careful of the broken ones, then sat in her new swing. With one foot, she set herself into motion.

"Do you like it?"

"Like it? Why . . . I think it's the most wonderful gift in the world." She shoved off once more. The movement stirred a breeze that ruffled her hair. Her smile was glorious.

Jake was content. He felt like a man who had wandered in the desert for six years and had suddenly come upon an oasis, cool, green, inviting. He stood in the yard, feeling the comfort of the oasis all around him.

And then he got greedy. He wanted to grab great handfuls of the oasis and stuff it into his pocket. He felt covetous. He wanted to possess. But he knew possession would mean destruction.

"Jake." Sarah called to him, laughing. "Come join me." She patted the wooden slats beside her.

Need made him take one step toward her; caution made him pull back.

"Enjoy the swing, Sarah. There's something I have to do."

"You're leaving?"

He was selfish; he loved the disappointment in her voice.

"No, I'm going to repair your porch steps."

"I'll help."

He pictured Sarah, standing beside him, her skirt brushing against his leg. He couldn't endure it.

"No. You need to watch after Jenny."

"She's sleeping." She left her swing. Jake couldn't stand to be near her and not touch her.

"Stay," he said, harsher than he meant to. Her eyes widened. "Please," he said gently, smiling. "I want to watch you enjoying my gift."

"In that case . . ." Sarah returned to the swing and set it into motion.

With a safe distance separating them, Jake began

to work and Sarah began to talk. He loved the music of her voice. It was a cool wind, blowing across the oasis.

"You're spoiling me, Jake."

"That's what friends are for."

"I probably should be inside sewing. . . ."

"Stay . . . please."

Their gazes touched, softly, then drifted apart. He hammered and she swung.

"I guess you think I was silly . . . dancing with a mop."

"No."

"I love to dance. Sometimes I dream about wearing a real dance dress with a swirly skirt, about dancing with a real band . . . in the arms of a real man."

He silenced the hammer; she brought the swing to a stop. Something shimmered in the air between them, something that warmed his heart and lifted his spirit.

Laughing self-consciously, Sarah fussed with her hair.

"Just listen to me, prattling on about myself." She twisted a curl around her finger. "Tell me about your dreams, Jake."

"My dreams are dead."

He was sorry the minute he said it.

"I'm sorry," she said.

"Don't be."

He swung the hammer viciously. He could feel Sarah watching him. Ghosts grabbed at his mind. Darkness seeped into his spirit. He dared not look at Sarah.

She set the swing back in motion. Her feet tapped lightly against the porch floor, and the chains anchoring the swing squeaked. Still, Jake couldn't look at her. He had admitted to dead dreams. He had made himself vulnerable.

Sweat trickled down his neck and into the collar of his shirt. He wasn't dressed for hard labor. He had acted on impulse, knowing from experience how often impulse led to regret.

Sarah's swing grew still, and so did his hammer. The careful silence set his nerves on edge. Sarah rescued him.

"I must check on Jenny."

"Yes," he said, without looking at her. Then, feeling a coward, he looked into her face. It was serene, unreadable. "Sarah, I'll be leaving as soon as I finish here."

"I understand."

She left quietly, her footsteps echoing on the wooden porch. When the screen door closed behind her, he threw the hammer to the ground, cursing softly.

Gwendolyn had been wise to warn him. The pity was that he hadn't heeded her warning. Worse, he hadn't followed his own instincts. He should have told Sarah good-bye when he'd first stepped into her Dollhouse. Now it was too late.

He picked the hammer up and attacked the sagging steps, his mind alive with dark thoughts.

Six

"You're in a black mood today, Jake," Gwendolyn told him.

"Black is my favorite color."

"I see the afternoon off yesterday didn't improve your temper." He didn't comment. Gwendolyn was not deterred. "You didn't tell her good-bye, did you?"

Instead of answering, Jake stared out the window, seeing not the tree-shaded recreation area of Townsend Publishing but rather a woman with bright golden hair, sitting in a porch swing. Sarah Love consumed him.

"Jake?" Gwendolyn had come to stand beside him, and her voice was soft. Gently she put a hand on his shoulder. "Can I help you?"

Briefly he closed his eyes. An agony of indecision tore at him.

"I'm damned if I leave her and damned if I don't, Gwendolyn." He took the liver-spotted hand that rested on his shoulder and kissed it. "I'm in too deep to back out now." He lifted haunted eyes to Gwendolyn's face. She had tears on her cheeks. "I can't just walk out of their lives. Not yet. They *need* me."

Gwendolyn wiped the tears off her cheeks, then stiffened her spine and marched to the chair in front of her desk.

"Hell, Jake, this hearts-and-flowers routine has got me bawling like a baby." She flipped open her steno pad and glared at him. "So . . . they *need* you. Then get off your duff and figure out how you can help them—besides painting and mowing the lawn and fixing the porch steps. Have I missed anything?"

"Not a thing." *Except the way Sarah smiles, the way she tells me her dreams, the way she tells me I'm a hero.* "Do you know how to baby-sit, Gwendolyn?"

"I take it this is not an idle question."

"No."

"I'd sit with a baby Godzilla if you asked me, Jake." She smoothed the front of her dress. "Kindness doesn't motivate me, you understand. Greed does. I'd charge you a fortune."

"Good. I'll pay it. For Jenny." He laughed. Then he stood up and began to pace.

"We're having a benefit dance," he said.

"Benefiting what?"

"Special children."

"Where and when?"

"Next weekend. My house."

"Next weekend? Have you gone crazy?"

"Probably. I want a live band, a good one, and I want you to select a dress, a pretty one, blue, I think . . . yes, blue. Size . . . um . . . six. Send it to Sarah Love. Send roses too. Yellow. Call in a few favors. Get the invitations printed *today*. The secretarial pool can help you address them."

He could picture Sarah, a blue dress swirling around her legs, her head tilted back to smile up at her dance partner, her hero. *Him.* Caught up in his dream, Jake paced, smiling and nodding with satisfaction.

He couldn't leave Sarah, not yet, not until she and Jenny were firmly established in Florence society. In the meantime, what would it hurt if he gave her a dream?

Sarah had her head bent over her sewing, stitching and dreaming. Beside her, Jenny hummed as she painted doll faces.

Her shop bell rang.

"Come in."

A young man with a shy smile, two enormous boxes, and a bouquet of yellow roses walked through her door.

"Are you Ms. Sarah Love?"

"Yes."

"I got some packages for you."

"For me?"

"That's what the card says: Ms. Sarah Love."

Jake, her mind whispered. *Jake.* But why? She had last seen him standing on her front porch with a hammer in his hand, his face dark and brooding. That encounter had started off like a swan ride through an enchanted lake and had ended like a roller-coaster ride through a tunnel of despair.

She looked at the yellow roses. Jake had brought Jenny a yellow rose. Her heart hammered so hard, she felt breathless.

"Ma'am?"

The delivery boy was standing in her doorway, a puzzled look on his face. She had to do something.

Pretending a nonchalance she didn't feel, she took the packages and the roses.

"Thank you."

"You're most welcome, ma'am." He tipped his hat and backed out her door. She gripped the packages, watching until he was out of sight.

"Pretty," Jenny said, looking up at the roses.

Her daughter's voice brought her back to reality. "Yes, Jenny. These are pretty flowers. From Jake."

She didn't have to look at the card to know. She placed the packages on a table while she put the roses in water. She leaned over, inhaling their fragrance; then she pressed her face against the petals. The last thing she did was look at the card. *Jake,* it said. Nothing more. Not best wishes, greetings, have a nice day. Just Jake.

"Mine," Jenny said, reaching for the boxes.

"Wait, Jenny. Let me see."

The boxes were wrapped in silver paper and tied with blue ribbon. The small box was for Jenny, the large box for her. Sarah ran her hands over the wrappings, savoring the moment, stretching out the anticipation.

"Oh, Jake," she whispered. "Why do you keep giving gifts?" *I give for my own pleasure,* he had said. *And for mine,* she added to herself.

"Mine, mine," Jenny chanted impatiently.

"Yes, Jenny. This one is for you." Sarah set her own package aside and helped Jenny open hers.

It was a Pooh Bear and a set of A. A. Milne books. Sarah read the card aloud. "Dear Jenny, I have a very good friend named Gwendolyn who loves to read *Winnie the Pooh* books to good little girls like you. Save the books for her to read to you Saturday night. Jake."

Jenny hugged her bear, whispering, " 'ake, 'ake."

Her heart pounding now, Sarah opened the other box. A beautiful blue dance dress lay among the folds of tissue paper.

"Oh." Sarah touched the dress with her fingertips, hardly daring to believe what she saw. Her own blood hummed in her ears until she felt almost dizzy.

She picked up the card and began to read: "Blue becomes you. Wear the dress for me, please. Saturday night at eight. I'll have my executive assistant, Gwendolyn, with me. You can leave Jenny in her care with complete confidence. Jake."

Another mystery. Another surprise.

Sarah pressed the dress to her cheek. "Oh, Jake. Don't make me fall in love with you."

"I don't know how I got talked into this," Gwendolyn grumbled as she and Jake approached Sarah's house.

"It was your idea."

"*My* idea?"

"Yes. And stop complaining. Nobody in this car thinks you mean it."

"Hmmph. I have to complain. I'd ruin my image otherwise." Gwendolyn smoothed the front of her dress. "Do I look all right?"

"Jenny will love you."

And she did. She was waiting behind the door with her Pooh Bear and her books and her puppy. Two minutes after Gwendolyn entered the room, she and Jenny were fast friends.

Sarah, serene and beautiful in her blue dress, stood beside the sofa watching her daughter. She looked as reserved as Jake felt.

All week he had anticipated this evening. Now that it had arrived, he found himself wondering what he would do. Sarah was not just any woman. When he was with her, even the most casual touch had a way of getting out of hand.

His gaze roamed over her. The blue dress left her shoulders bare. They were as creamy and soft looking as he had imagined. Nothing dark and hard and angular about Sarah Love.

"Ready?" he asked.

"Yes."

Sarah took his arm almost shyly. He led her to the car and helped her in, keeping a careful rein on his emotions.

"Comfortable?"

She smiled. "Yes. Thank you." He almost drowned in her blue eyes.

Feeling generous and noble, he slid into the driver's seat, whistling. The engine purred to life when he turned the key, and they slid smoothly onto the road. Night caught them in its dark embrace. Sarah sat beside him like a dream, softly illuminated by the dashboard lights. The tires whispered on the pavement, and outside a cloud covered the moon.

"What is that song?" Sarah asked.

"'La Vie en Rose.'" He hadn't been aware until she asked.

"Edith Piaf."

"You know her?"

"Yes. Her music is beautiful."

Love songs. He was whistling love songs. Jake stopped whistling.

"Looks like it might storm," he said. Talking about the weather. He must be getting desperate. It was too early in the evening to get desperate.

"I hope not. There's something primitive about a storm, something almost frightening."

A storm took Bonnie away. Change the subject.

Sarah changed it for him. "You never told me where we are going."

"Do you trust me, Sarah?"

"Yes. I trust you." She spoke without hesitation. He hadn't realized until he'd asked the question, until she had answered, how much he wanted her trust.

He turned the car onto his street.

"We're going to your house?" There was no question in Sarah's voice, no fear.

"Yes." As they turned up his driveway he pressed the button to lower the car windows. He wanted her to hear the music before he told her about the dance.

The first faint strains of orchestra music came to them, borne on the night wind. Sarah cocked her head, listening.

"Is that music I hear?"

"That's a full-fledged orchestra."

"You're having a party . . . with a real orchestra?"

"A benefit dance for special children."

"Oh, Jake . . . because of Jenny?"

"Because of Jenny." *And you.*

He parked the car, and Sarah reached across the seat to squeeze his hand. "How can I ever thank you?" Her eyes were bright with unshed tears.

He cupped her cheek, briefly, tenderly. Then he let go. He *had* to.

"You can thank me by smiling." Her smile put the sun to shame. "And by enjoying every dance."

"If they're all with you, I will."

Jake let that remark slide. He didn't dare reply. He didn't dare even think about the meaning.

"Are you ready to go inside, Sarah?"

"Oh, yes, Jake. A real dance . . . I can hardly wait."

"You'll be meeting lots of people—very fine people." He helped her from the car. In the moonlight she looked like fine porcelain. Men would fawn over her, fight for her attentions. Already he was jealous. And furious at himself for his jealousy.

He took her arm and led her up the front steps. The carved double doors loomed before them, an entry into another world for Sarah.

"Save your last dance for me, Sarah," he said, just before he opened the door.

"I'll save all my dances for you."

It was a beautiful dream, Sarah saving all her dances for him, a dream he dared not believe in. Aching with both tenderness and fear, he led her through the door.

The party was in full swing. Sarah felt as if she had entered a fantasy world. Music soared around her, blending with the sounds of laughter and the tinkling of champagne glasses. The crowd moved in waves, like brightly colored streamers caught in a summer wind.

For a while she could do nothing except stand and stare. Jake gave her arm a reassuring squeeze.

"You're the most beautiful woman here."

"Hold on to me, Jake. Don't let go yet."

"You're not afraid, are you?"

"No. I'm . . . overwhelmed."

The last time she had danced, she had been inside a smoky nightclub with Bobby Wayne, three months before their marriage. The band had been country-and-western and the drink of choice bourbon.

Sarah had no more time to remember her last dance, for several people in the crowd broke away and came toward them. Jake introduced Sarah to all of them. Their names began to run together.

"Who is that beautiful dark-haired woman coming our way?" Sarah asked.

"Hallie Donovan Butler, with her husband Josh. She's the founder of the theater for special children here in Florence."

Hallie descended on them, both hands extended. "Jake, welcome back. I was beginning to think we had lost you, you big old cuddle bum." Still holding one of his hands, she turned to Sarah. "And you must be Sarah Love. Tell me all about yourself."

Sarah found Hallie charming as well as easy to talk to.

"What did she mean about losing you?" she asked, after Hallie and her husband left.

"I haven't been a very visible member of society for a while."

Why, Sarah wanted to ask, but a new group of people besieged them. Jake chatted easily, keeping his hand on Sarah's back, all the while leading her toward the dance floor.

"Can I claim the first dance, Sarah, before half the bachelors in Florence capture you?"

Jake pulled her into his arms. She felt as if she had been waiting all her life for just this moment. Sheltered in his arms with music flowing around her, she felt safe, secure, and cherished. Though why she should feel cherished by a man who had never pledged anything except friendship, she didn't know.

She closed her eyes, losing herself in the beauty of the music and the nearness of Jake. And when the song was over, he didn't let go. There was no more talk of being captured by Florence's bachelors, no more talk of saving the last dance for him.

All the dances were for him. She knew it, and he knew it. Hour after hour the music gave them an excuse to hold each other close. They didn't speak. Words might have ruined the magic.

When the last note died away and the last guest left the house, Sarah and Jake realized what they had done.

"I monopolized you," he said, his face tight.

"I'm glad."

"Are you?" His eyes were full of promises almost too wonderful to be true.

She cupped his cheeks. "Yes, Jake. Very glad." She was so close to falling in love, so very close. Any other time, any other place she might have exercised caution, might have cited reasons. But for this night she was in another world, a world filled with mystery and magic and endless possibilities.

He leaned toward her, and she lifted her face. The kiss was inevitable. Their fate had been sealed the moment they'd danced the first dance.

The kiss started sweet and tender. She stood on tiptoe, winding her arms tighter around his neck.

"Oh, Jake," she whispered.

"Sarah?" His eyes were very dark. "My Sarah." He held her so tightly, she could barely breathe.

Outside, the first crack of lightning split the air. Thunder rolled through the summer clouds, scattering them across the sullen sky.

She felt the tremor that ran through Jake. She held on tighter, running her hands over his tense back, whispering his name, over and over.

Suddenly he lifted her in his arms and started toward the stairs. His jaw was tight, his eyes blazing. She knew where he was taking her, knew his intent.

"Say you don't want this, Sarah," he said, his foot resting on the first stair. "Tell me to stop."

"No. Don't stop."

Storm winds raged against the house, rattling the

windowpanes. A muscle in Jake's jaw twitched. His eyes were haunted. Resolutely he climbed the stairs.

"Save yourself from me, Sarah. Say no."

"You need me, Jake. Tonight will be my gift to you."

"I didn't want to buy you."

"You didn't buy me. I'm giving myself freely."

At the top of the stairs, he gazed fiercely into her face. "This is need, Sarah. And hunger. Nothing more."

"I understand." She cupped her face and pressed her lips to his. *This is love, Jake.*

All the pent-up need in him came pouring forth in the kiss. Sarah wound her hands in his hair, holding on so he wouldn't let go, holding on so she wouldn't lose him.

Outside the rains lashed the roof, and the winds moaned against the eaves. Jake seemed to have captured nature's turmoil in his soul. His kisses were hard, harsh, demanding.

"Don't be afraid, Sarah. Don't be afraid of the storm," he murmured as he carried her into his bedroom and kicked the door shut.

Sarah hadn't thought to be afraid of the storm raging outside. The thing she feared was the storm raging inside herself. What she was about to do would change the course of her life. After this night she knew she could never view Jake as merely a friend. *Need* and *hunger,* he had said. She had needs, too, needs that only Jake could awaken, a hunger that only he could satisfy.

As he lowered her to the bed she thought fleetingly of Jenny. *Forgive me, Jenny. Tonight I need a dream. Tonight I need Jake.* She would be sensible tomorrow.

He undressed her with a slow and tender reverence surprising coming from a man so fierce.

"You are exquisite." He traced her body with his hands. She shivered with pleasure. Until that moment she hadn't realized how she had longed for Jake to consider her beautiful.

He spread her hair upon the pillow, watching it catch the glow from the single lamp burning beside his bed.

"Your hair . . ." He let the strands sift through his fingers. "I could spend the rest of the night worshiping your hair." Leaning close, he brushed his lips down the side of her throat. "If there weren't so much more I wanted to worship"—his voice became husky as he kissed the tops of her breasts—"so much more I want to possess."

Jake began to kiss her body, slowly, purposefully, and with great skill. Passion and tenderness vied for dominance until they merged into one emotion Sarah could only describe as glory. Glory covered her, claimed her, filled her. It had a name, and its name was Jake.

"Jake," she whispered, time and again, longing, hoping, waiting, yearning. . . .

"Not yet, Sarah. Not yet."

Outside the window, the elements were at war. Thunder and lightning clashed in the sky; wind and rain lashed the house. As the storm gathered force, so did Jake's passion. His mouth and hands burned over her, seared her.

Sarah had no concept of time. There was only the moment, and Jake filled it until nothing existed except the passion that flamed between them.

A flash of lightning illuminated his face. It was dark, brooding, dangerous. With an insight given to those who love, Sarah understood that when Jake warned her against the storm, he had been warning her against himself.

A shiver ran through her, and she couldn't name its source. Love? Passion? Hope? Fear? Tomorrow would be time enough to know, she thought. For tonight she had Jake, only Jake.

He raised himself on his elbows and looked down at her. "Say you want me, Sarah."

"I want you."

His eyes darkened; his face was unfathomable. "I *need* you, Sarah. Heaven help me, I need you."

"Jake." She lifted her arms. There would be no turning back. "Come to me."

There was no tenderness in their joining. With a harsh cry that matched the storm, Jake claimed Sarah. When he had first kissed her, stars sprinkled her soul. When he possessed her, the heavens emptied themselves, so that everything bright and wondrous and awesome came together in her heart.

Sarah was afraid if she breathed too deeply, Jake might vanish. If she blinked her eyes, she might find herself in the middle of a dream, clutching nothing but thin air.

There might never be another moment like this, she thought, holding Jake close. His great need poured forth in his lovemaking. Sarah took that need and cherished it. All that was beautiful in her, all that was gentle, all that was warm, tried to reach from her heart to his. But the chasm was too deep, the gap too wide.

Oh, Jake. What demons drive you?

"Sarah! Sarah!" His cry was harsh rather than exultant, haunted rather than free.

She wrapped her arms around his sweat-slickened body, whispering his name. With one final cry he ended the sweet torment.

He lay against her, his breathing heavy. She caressed his damp back, murmuring words brought up from her soul.

"Jake . . . my sweet . . . my dear."

He lay very still, his breathing gradually becoming steady.

His silence tore at her, even as the storm ripped at the windows. *Say something*, she wanted to scream. *Anything.*

Her hands moved over his back. "Jake . . ." Still he was silent. She could feel the rhythm of his heart slowing. "My hero . . ." she whispered. "My love."

His eyes blazed as he lifted himself off her. "What have I done to you, Sarah. . . . What have I done?"

She lifted one hand toward him, but he stood up and moved out of her reach.

"Jake, please, tell me what's wrong?"

She sat up, pulling the sheet around her.

He leaned down, and for a moment she thought he was going to take her in his arms. She thought he would smile and say everything was all right.

Anxiety marched through her, wearing combat boots. Sarah shivered. Jake's face was troubled as he stood beside the bed looking down at her. He reached toward her, then quickly withdrew his hand.

Silence screamed around them, tearing at Sarah's nerves. Thunder and lightning cracked the heavens, but she imagined it was her heart.

"Oh, Jake . . . please . . ."

"Forgive me, Sarah."

He left her in the bed among the tumbled covers.

Seven

Jake shut himself in the bathroom and leaned against the sink. A giant hand was squeezing all the breath from him.

He threw back his head and gulped air, trying to relieve the smothering feeling. He had taken Sarah like the lowest beast in the jungle. He had used her to relieve his own desperate need, used her and then tossed her aside as if she were a rag doll.

"Bastard," he whispered.

The storm tore at his windows. Jake clenched his hands into fists and shook them at the storm.

It's the damned storm, the storm that makes me destroy.

Sweat poured off his body, and he knew it was more than the result of exertion: It was the sweat of fear. He passed his hands over his eyes, as if the gesture would clear his mind.

A vision of Sarah came to him, a golden vision of soft skin and luscious curves and sweet warm yielding flesh that had driven him almost insane. *Need*, he had said. He had needed her.

He leaned his face into his hands and groaned. Need had driven him to her arms, propelled him up the stairs and into the bed. Need had removed her clothes and kissed her lips and tasted her breasts. Need had entered that glorious body and begun the long journey through the stormy night. But it hadn't been need that performed the final act of surrender. It hadn't been passion that had spilled its seed. It had been love.

"Nooo," Jake moaned. Once more he shook his clenched fists at the storm. He couldn't love Sarah, *wouldn't* love her. To love her was to destroy her.

Wind shook the windows, and he felt its chill blow across his heart. What was Sarah doing now? Was she lying in the bed where he had abandoned her, crying her eyes out? Was her lush body still curved under the sheet? Was she waiting, naked, for him to return.

He didn't think he could face her after what he had done. *Coward,* his mind whispered.

Jake splashed cold water on his face, then wrapped a towel around his waist. He had to go back. He couldn't take back what he had done, but he could offer some explanation. Sarah deserved some sort of truth.

Resolutely he opened the bathroom door, then stood in the bedroom, adjusting his eyes to the dimness. Sarah was standing beside the window, fully dressed, looking out at the storm. If she heard him come back, she gave no indication.

Good. He reached for his clothes and dressed quickly and quietly. Still, Sarah didn't turn from the window. Her stance, stiff and proud, pierced his heart. *I've hurt her.* The part of him that hoped, the part that had been struggling to be reborn, died a quiet death.

He crossed the room and put his hands on her shoulders. She trembled.

"Sarah . . . Look at me, Sarah."

When she turned, he saw the stains on her cheeks. *Tears.* She had been crying. He bit back a curse.

"It's all right, Jake." She put her hand on his cheek, smiling bravely. "Really, it is."

"No. I hurt you . . . I never meant to hurt you."

"You didn't . . . what we had was beautiful."

"What I did was selfish." He saw forgiveness in her eyes, forgiveness and a willingness to go on as they were. He couldn't continue to take advantage of her kindness. He released her, then stepped back.

"There is something I have to tell you, Sarah. Something I have to explain."

"You don't owe me any explanations. You made everything perfectly clear before . . ." Color flooded her cheeks and she fussed at her hair. "And anyhow, I can't possibly commit myself to a relationship . . . with you or anyone else. I have Jenny—"

"Sarah." His gentle command stopped her rush of words. "Please, sit down."

She sat on the edge of a wingback chair and folded her hands in her lap. Except for the flush on her cheeks and the brightness in her eyes, she didn't look like a woman who had recently been loved.

Not loved. Used. He had to keep that distinction clear in his mind. What he had felt might have been love, but what he had done was not.

"I was married once, Sarah." She sucked in her breath. "Her name was Michelle."

"Jake," Sarah said, leaning forward in her chair. "You don't have to tell me this."

"Please . . ." He held up his hand, and she fell silent. "We met in New Orleans. She was looking for a good time, and so was I. My daughter was conceived that night. . . . Bonnie."

Sarah remained silent. He didn't dare look at her. Instead, he gazed out the window. The worst of the storm was over, but wind still howled around the eaves.

"Michelle wanted to have an abortion. I wouldn't hear of it." His hands tightened into fists as he remembered. "It was a marriage that never should have been, a marriage doomed to failure."

"You have a child?"

"Had. Bonnie is dead. I killed her."

"No!" Sarah was out of her chair. She ran to him and caught his arms. "You couldn't have. You're not capable of such a thing."

He gazed down at Sarah, seeing the trust in her eyes, the need to believe in him. He couldn't let her hope. It would be cruel.

"We were trapped, Michelle and I. Divorce was out of the question. Neither of us wanted to lose Bonnie." He gently removed Sarah's hands and stepped out of her reach. "We learned to hate. Finally Michelle could stand it no more."

He could hear distant thunder. The wind picked up speed, until it seemed to be seeping through every crevice, spreading its discontent throughout his house. In spite of summer, Jake felt chilled.

"Jake . . . please." Sarah caught his arm again and forced him to look at her. "Don't do this to yourself."

"I have to tell you, Sarah . . . I have to make you understand . . ." He didn't finish the sentence. *Understand my motives. Understand my pain. Understand my fear.* He hoped she knew.

"Then tell me what happened. I will listen, but I won't judge." Sarah returned to her chair.

The dignity he had come to love had never been more in evidence. For a moment Jake was tempted to take her in his arms and carry her back to the bed. He was tempted to give up the past, forget about the future, and merely savor the moment.

But he held firm. He couldn't hold on to her. He didn't dare.

"It was storming that night," he continued. "We had a terrible fight. Michelle said she was leaving, that I could have Bonnie. She just wanted out." He closed his eyes, trying to block out the pain, but it came along with the memories. "She had her bags already packed. I said I would drive her to a motel."

Words got caught in his throat. Jake began to pace. Intermittent flashes of lightning illuminated Sarah's face. She had gone very pale.

"The roads were treacherous . . . because of the storm. I took a curve too fast. The car flipped over and over, landing bottom side up."

Sarah made a small sound of horror. She started to rise from her chair, but the look on his face stopped her.

"Michelle was killed instantly. . . .Bonnie took longer to die."

"Bonnie?" Sarah's voice was no more than a whisper, but he could hear the horror.

"Apparently she'd heard us quarreling. She hid in the backseat of the car with her blanket and her teddy bear."

"Oh, Jake, no . . . I'm so sorry."

Tears streamed down Sarah's face now, unchecked, but she didn't rise from her chair. What woman in her right mind would? What woman would offer comfort to a murderer? Jake had to finish the story. He couldn't spare himself now.

"I was holding Bonnie in my arms when she died three days later at the hospital."

Death had entered the room. The silence that enveloped Jake and Sarah was resonant with ghosts. Sarah cried silently, and Jake stood beside the window, hurting.

He longed to comfort Sarah, to tell her that everything would be all right. But his comfort would be even more cruel than his brutal honesty. Comfort would give false hope. He wouldn't give himself false hope, and he wouldn't give it to Sarah.

Sarah's tears shone in the lamplight. She watched him as she cried. He searched for horror in her face, but didn't find it. He searched for love, and couldn't see it.

"How you must have suffered," she said quietly.

"I don't want your pity." He was harsh with her, but he excused himself on the grounds that harshness kills hope.

"It's not pity I feel, Jake. It's compassion."

"I killed them. I deserve to suffer."

"No!" She started toward him. He could almost feel her arms around his waist, feel her head upon his chest. It was Sarah's way of giving comfort. But he had to refuse all comfort—for both their sakes.

"It's over, Sarah." His harsh words brought her to a halt.

He saw her gather her courage, saw the emotional toll it took on her. His dark destiny seemed to be hurting women.

"What about Jenny?" There was no tremor in her voice, no note of pleading.

"I've hurt you, Sarah. I won't hurt her too."

"What does that mean? Does that mean you won't hurt her by leaving or you won't hurt her by staying?"

Jake was relieved to see her anger. It was a good

antidote to pain. It also meant that Sarah would survive. He had hurt her, but he hadn't damaged her beyond repair.

"I won't abandon her . . . not yet. Soon the summer will be over. She'll be in school, make new friends."

"You're leaving, then."

"Yes . . . eventually. I'll ease out of Jenny's life. She'll never even know I've gone."

"You're wrong, but I can't force you to stay."

"I'm glad you understand."

"No! I don't understand any of this." Sarah paced, her hands folded tightly together. "I don't understand how you can blame yourself for an accident. I don't understand why you won't accept compassion. I don't understand the wall you've built around yourself." She paused, gazing toward the bed. "And most of all . . . I don't understand what happened there."

"Neither do I."

Sarah lifted her chin and gazed defiantly into his eyes. "Take me home, Jake."

They didn't touch as they left the room, didn't talk as they descended the staircase. Jake stopped in the front hall and got a large raincoat from the closet. Still without speaking, he wrapped it around Sarah.

His hands brushed against her bare shoulders. She shivered, but that was the only sign she gave of emotional turmoil.

When he opened the door, the last of the storm winds tore at them. Jake took Sarah's arm. She stiffened.

"The sidewalks are slick," he explained. "I don't want you to fall."

She didn't pull away, but she was stiff and unyielding. That alone told him how much he had hurt her.

By nature Sarah was loving and generous, warm and spontaneous, compassionate and forgiving.

He drove slowly and carefully, his hands gripping the wheel until his knuckles were white. Sarah sat quietly beside him. Her dignity shamed him.

The storm had abated by the time they reached her house, but a light rain still fell. He escorted her to her door. She had left the porch light burning.

As she fitted her key into the lock she looked at him. In her face he saw hope that he had killed, love he had denied, pain that he had caused. A vision of raw earth, piled into two fresh mounds, came to his mind. Standing on the porch, bearing Sarah's scrutiny, he felt as if he had killed something beautiful inside her. And he was ashamed.

"Sarah." He reached out, wanting to touch her. But in the end, he drew his hand back. "I'm sorry."

"Don't . . ." She turned her back to him and busied herself with the door. "You're right. It's over."

Gwendolyn was sitting on the sofa, reading a book. She stood up when they came in. Her expression changed from welcoming to wise. Quietly, she closed her book.

"Jenny's a love. We had a great time, and now she's sound asleep."

"Thank you, Gwendolyn."

"Anytime, Sarah."

Jake hovered in the doorway like a dark angel. Sarah stood in the middle of the room, scrupulously avoiding looking his way. Gwendolyn glanced from one to the other, started to say something else, then changed her mind.

"Are you ready to go, Gwendolyn?"

"Whenever you are, Jake . . . well . . . good night, Sarah."

"Good night."

Still, Sarah didn't look at him. There was nothing he could say to repair the damage he had done. In the end he left without saying good-bye.

He heard Sarah lock the door behind him. Gwendolyn turned to him.

"Well?"

"Don't say anything, Gwendolyn."

"How can I keep quiet? You two left looking like Prince Charming taking Cinderella to the ball, and you came back looking like Dracula and his bride. What the hell happened?"

Jake took her elbow and propelled her toward the car.

"I wanted to give her a dream, and I ended up giving her a nightmare."

Sarah stood behind the door, listening for the sound of Jake's car. Finally it came, out of the darkness. He was leaving. And he wouldn't be back . . . not in his usual way. There would be no exchanged glances, no spontaneous laughter, no precious moments of uninhibited joy.

Leaning against the door, she shivered and pulled Jake's coat around her. She had forgotten to give it back. She would do that as quickly as possible. She wanted no physical reminders of him.

She took the coat off and folded it carefully. Jake's scent was caught in the heavy fabric. Such longing seized Sarah that she had to sit down.

The pain of loving a dark, unapproachable man almost overwhelmed her. She pressed her cheek to the coat. How could she have let tonight happen? she wondered. She had thought she was wise and brave. She had thought she knew the difference between dreams and reality. What had happened in Jake's bed had been a dream, an impossible dream, and for a moment she had allowed herself to believe it was real.

Her tears wet the coat, and she brushed frantically at them. She didn't want to stain his coat. She didn't want to stain his life.

Sarah stood up, carried the coat to her bedroom, and placed it on the top shelf of the closet, out of sight. She didn't want to see it hanging next to her clothes. She didn't want her dresses brushing against the coat. It would be too much like touching Jake.

Sarah removed her party dress and shook it out. She would send that back too. She had broken her own policy of not involving herself with men, and they were both paying a hard price for her foolishness.

Somehow she would pay for the lawn mowing, too, and the repair to her front steps. She wasn't a charity case . . . and Jake was no longer her friend.

Sarah climbed into bed and pulled the sheets close to her chin. She would have covered her head if that would have solved anything. But she knew it wouldn't.

For a long time she lay staring into the darkness. *Jake, Jake.* His name whispered through her mind. *My lost friend . . . my lost love.*

Jake's mood matched his house. Both were dark and forbidding. He started stripping his wet clothes off as he climbed the stairway. When he reached the bedroom, he stood looking in. Sarah was everywhere—in the rumpled covers, in the glow of the lamp, beside the window, in the chair. Her fragrance still lingered in the room, and it was more than he could bear.

He went into a guest bedroom down the hall and climbed into bed. *Don't think about anything,* he ordered himself. But he couldn't heed his own advice. His thoughts tumbled around his mind like ninepins. Finally he gave up sleep and spent the rest of the night pacing.

"I hear you took to the sky yesterday," Gwendolyn said the minute he entered his office on Monday morning.

"I might as well post my activities in the newspaper." Jake didn't have to ask how Gwendolyn knew. She and Bert Donnogan had been friends for years. Lovers, too, he guessed, though neither of them had ever said so.

"Bert said you damn near killed yourself—twice."

"Bert scares easily."

Gwendolyn put both hands on his desk and leaned toward him. "Jake, don't keep doing this to yourself."

"Skydiving is a hobby, Gwendolyn, not something I'm doing to myself."

"You know what I'm talking about, and don't pretend you don't." She marched across the room and poured two cups of coffee, strong and black, the way they both liked it. Encased in her chair with her coffee, she glared at him.

"You can't keep blaming yourself for their deaths. You have more sense than that."

Refusing to be sucked into that conversation, he sipped his coffee. Gwendolyn was not deterred.

"Running away is easy. Isn't it, Jake?"

"Less than two weeks ago you recommended it."

"No, I didn't. I said don't use that child as a substitute. That's not the same at all."

He gave her a long, steady look. She didn't back down, but returned his study.

"Yes, Gwendolyn," he finally said. "Running away is easier . . . but it's the only option I have right now."

"If you really want to know what I think—"

Gwendolyn was interrupted by the postman. He stood in the doorway, his mail bag slung over his back, his hat in one hand and a large box in the other. Gwendolyn saw him first.

"Mr. Freeman . . . what in the world brings you up here? Is something wrong with our box downstairs?"

"No. Nothing like that." He cleared his throat and his Adam's apple bobbed up and down. "This is highly irregular . . . but she's such a nice little lady."

"She?" Jake turned toward the postman, fully alert.

"Ms. Love." Jake ached at the sound of her name. There was no escape. Wherever he was, there would always be reminders of what he had done.

"Sarah Love?" he asked.

"Yes, that sweet little woman on the other side of town. She asked me for a favor . . . and . . . well, I just couldn't turn her down."

"Is she in trouble?" The protective instinct propelled Jake across the room.

"No. Nothing like that. She asked me to bring this to you . . . along with the mail . . . and . . . well, I guess there's no harm."

"None at all." Jake took the package. "Thank you, Mr. Freeman."

"Well. See y'all." The postman tipped his hat and left.

After the door had closed behind him, Jake glared at Gwendolyn.

"Don't say a word."

"Who me?" She gathered her coffee cup and headed for the door. "I was just leaving."

Jake waited until she had gone to open the package. His raincoat was inside . . . and the blue dress. Sarah's fragrance wafted up from the box.

Jake clutched the box so hard, the sides began to cave in. Her note lay against the folds of the coat, accusing him. He stared at it a long time, unable to pick it up.

Slowly he laid the box aside and opened the note. It was handwritten.

"Dear Jake," it began. He closed his eyes, remembering the sound of her voice. *Jake . . . my dear, my hero, my love.*

He had to sit down. Bowing his head over the note, he closed his eyes. Love shouldn't hurt so much.

Finally he drew a deep breath and continued reading.

"I don't mean to seem ungrateful, but I'm returning the dress along with your coat. After what happened, it doesn't seem right to keep it."

"Sarah . . . Sarah," he whispered, remembering her in the blue dress. Her name echoed in the room like a soft summer breeze.

The chill of loss swept through him. Jake stared at the window, seeing nothing and remembering everything. Doubts crowded into his mind. How could he live, knowing he loved Sarah and could never have her?

"She's safe," he whispered. "At least now she's safe from me."

He turned his attention back to the note. "Please don't feel bad about what happened." How like Sarah to think of the other person. "I share the blame. I'm an adult, fully capable of making my own choices. I chose to be with you, Jake. Don't ever forget that. I *chose* to."

How could she have refused. He had practically dragged her up the steps before he'd even asked.

She had signed the note simply "Sarah." He traced the letters with his fingers. It was almost like touching her. Her essence seemed to be distilled in the note.

He folded the note carefully, put it in the left-hand drawer of his desk, and turned the key. Sarah was now locked away with his other memorabilia—a heart-shaped locket that had been Bonnie's, a locket that contained a strand of her dark hair.

He buzzed for Gwendolyn. "We have work to do, or have you forgotten that this is an office?"

Gwendolyn came in scowling. "I could run this company without you, Jake, and with one hand tied behind my back in the bargain. And don't you forget that."

Jake held on to the hope that things would soon get back to normal.

Eight

That hope was dashed two days later when Sarah's second message arrived. The envelope was at the bottom of the stack. He tore into it, and out fell a crisp twenty-dollar bill.

Clutching it in his hand, he read the note attached. "This is partial payment for mowing the yard. I'll send the rest later, as well as payment for repairing the steps. Sarah. P.S. Where shall I send the swing?"

Fury blocked everything from his vision except the money. He ripped it in half and threw it onto his desk. Then he stalked from his office.

Gwendolyn looked up when he passed her desk.

"Did somebody forget to tell me we're being attacked by a herd of crazy, rabid elephants, or is that just the normal face you use to scare old ladies into heart attacks?"

"What?" He glared down at her.

"Now that I have your attention . . ." She stood up and faced him nose to nose. "I saw the return address on that letter, and I can guess where you're going."

"Don't. It's none of your affair."

"When I'm about to get stuck with Mr. Wonderful from Deltafax, it is. He's coming in about ten minutes, Jake, and unless you want to come back and find him dead on this carpet, you'd better get back in that office."

"Dead?" Jake was finally getting back under control.

"Every time he has to wait for you, he chases me round my desk pawing at my fabulous body. I'm not up to that today. I have in mind killing him with the blunt end of the letter opener."

Jake didn't try to suppress his laughter. It felt good.

"Hark! What is that strange noise I hear?" Gwendolyn clutched her chest in mock terror. "Can it be? Is it? It is! Laughter from Mr. Gloom and Doom himself."

"All right, Gwendolyn." Jake stifled his laughter and pretended outrage. "You've proved your point." He headed back to his office, calling over his shoulder, "I'll keep my appointment with Mr. Wonderful, but the next time you interfere with me, prepare to pay the consequences."

"I'm quaking in my boots."

Sarah was worried about sending Jake the money. It seemed so cold. And yet, under the circumstances, what could she do?

Fortunately she didn't have time to brood over the matter. The citizens of Florence had discovered her doll shop, and customers filtered in and out. Between making and selling her dolls, plus taking care of Jenny, she hardly had a moment to brood.

Except at night. The nights were bad.

Her shop bell rang, and two customers came throug
the door.

"Yahoo . . ." A woman who looked like the fai
godmother in Jenny's Cinderella book, stuck he
head around the door. "Is this the Dollhouse?"

"Yes, it is."

The woman pulled her head back and said to he
companion, "This is it, Dora Mae. Come on in . .
and stop fussing. It was just a little old lizard." Th
white-haired woman came into the shop, laughin
"A lizard ran over Dora Mae's foot out there in you
yard, and you'd have thought it was a dragon." Sh
paused, looking around the shop. "My, my, it lool
like Santa's workshop in here."

Dora Mae came in behind her companion, a sho
skinny woman who walked with a strange gait an
constantly peered over her shoulder as if she we
looking for goblins.

"Come on in here, Dora Mae, and say hello to th
nice lady."

Dora Mae turned to smile, and Sarah's hea
stopped. She was looking into the face of a ve
special woman, a woman with Down's syndrome.

Her companion bustled forward. "Hi, I'm Mon
gomery . . . I know it's a crazy name for a lady . .
makes me sound like a boxer . . . and this is n
sister, Dora Mae."

Sarah took Dora Mae's hand between both of her
"I'm so glad to meet you. My name is Sarah Love."

"I want a doll," Dora Mae said. "A pretty doll for n
bed."

"We'll find something very special for you." Sara
blinked back tears and led the woman to her de
shelves. "Why don't we start here. If you don't fir
something you like, tell me, and I'll make one to you
specifications."

Dora Mae loved all the dolls. She picked up each one and cradled it like a child. Sarah stood patiently beside her, explaining how each doll came into being.

The shop bell tinkled. Sarah looked toward the door and straight into the eyes of Jake Townsend. Seeing him revived all the memories she was trying to bury, all the passion she was trying to deny.

He stood just inside the door, frozen there as if time had suddenly come to a halt. His face was closed and dark, but it was his eyes that held her attention longest. They were very bright and alive with emotion.

Sarah pressed the doll she was holding against her chest. She was speechless, and, apparently, so was he. They stood for a long moment, regarding each other; then he closed the door and slipped into the shop. He came toward her, but stopped on the opposite side of the doll shelves.

Beside her, Dora Mae and Montgomery chattered about the dolls. Sarah nodded and smiled, pretending to be interested, but she didn't hear a word they said. Her mind was full of Jake.

Why had he come back? Memories of the last time they were together flooded over her. She could almost taste his mouth, hear his voice as he told her she was exquisite. Desire made her skin tingle.

She stared between the shelves. A large portion of his chest and the bottom half of his face were in her line of vision. She concentrated on his lips, on their shape, their remembered texture.

If she leaned down toward Dora Mae and slanted her eyes sideways, she realized she could see all of Jake's face. Up this close, his eyes were startlingly green. She forgot to breathe as she studied his face.

Suddenly she found him staring back at her. She straightened quickly and turned back to her customers. Her blood raced so hard, she could hear roaring in her ears.

She wondered if she was going to faint. Wouldn't that be ridiculous? *Chin up, Sarah,* she chided herself. She was not the fainting type, and she wasn't about to start now.

"I like this one."

"What?" Sarah said.

Montgomery handed her a doll. "My sister likes this one."

"I'm so glad. I'll put it in a box for her."

Dora Mae hugged the doll and watched her sister.

"Can she just carry it out like that?" Montgomery asked.

"Certainly." Sarah headed toward the front of her shop, where she had set up a small desk and her account books.

She had to pass by Jake. Although she scrupulously avoided looking his way, she could feel his gaze on her. She held her back very straight. *It's over,* she told herself all the way to her desk.

But the minute she turned around and saw him she knew she was lying. Maybe she would never be in his arms again, never feel his touch, never hear him whisper her name, but what they had shared was not over, would never be over. Not as long as she had breath in her body and a store of memories in her mind.

Her hands shook as she took Montgomery's money. "Thank you," she said. "Please do come again."

"Why, we certainly will. Dora Mae just loves the shop. Do you mind if we just come to look?"

"Of course not." The back of Sarah's neck prickled. She dared not look across the room at Jake.

The sisters left with their doll, and Sarah bent over her account book. She had to record her sale, and she took her time doing it.

"You have to look up sometime, Sarah." There was a tenderness in his voice that almost undid her.

Slowly she lifted her gaze to his. "Hello, Jake."

"Hello, Sarah."

Neither of them moved. The dolls watched them with painted eyes. Sarah wondered if they noticed how much like a hero Jake looked.

"You look good," he finally said.

"So do you." She held on to her pen as if it were a life raft and she were about to sink to the bottom of the ocean. They watched each other silently until Sarah could no longer stand the suspense. "Why did you come?"

"This." In three strides he was across the room, standing in front of her desk. He pulled a twenty-dollar bill from his pocket and laid it on her desk.

"That's for mowing the lawn," she said.

"Money can't buy my services, Sarah." His eyes held hers.

"I never meant to insult you, Jake, nor to shame you."

"You did neither. You made a mistake."

She had made a number of mistakes. Her first was letting Jake into her life; her second was letting him into her heart.

"I merely wanted you to understand that I'm independent. I can take care of myself and Jenny."

"Not by paying me, you won't. Everything I gave you is yours to keep, Sarah."

"I can't."

"You will." He leaned across the desk and caught her shoulders. Her insides melted at his touch, but she didn't let him know. She brought her chin up defiantly.

"Don't push this issue, Jake. My mind is made up."

"You can send all the money you want, Sarah. Send

it by the postman, send it in the mail, send it b
carrier pigeon if you like." He leaned closer, so clos
his breath stirred her hair and caressed her cheek
"You'll just be wasting your time." He tightened hi
hold on her. "I'll return it all . . . in person."

He captured her in a fierce stare. She bit the insid
of her bottom lip to keep it from trembling. Jake wa
angry, but it wasn't rage that made her tremble: I
was desire. Passion welled up so quickly in her, sh
wanted to scream.

He saw what was happening. The light of recogni
tion leaped to life in the center of his eyes. Sarah'
heart thudded and her knees trembled. Suddenl
there didn't seem to be enough air in the room. Sh
thought she might smother.

Closing her eyes, she took a deep breath.

"Sarah?" The tenderness in Jake's voice made he
open her eyes. His hold on her changed to a caress
"Sarah . . ." He brushed his mouth across hers.

All her hard-earned control vanished. All her reso
lutions fell by the wayside. How could she resist him

She circled her arms around his waist and drev
him close. He tangled his hands in her hair. Sh
tipped her face up to him, and he gazed down at her
They stood that way for an eternity.

When her nerves were tingling so hard she though
she might snap in two, Jake kissed her. There wa
such tenderness and longing in his kiss that sh
almost forgot who she was, who Jake was. They wer
two wounded people who didn't belong together, wh
could never be together.

But, oh, loving him felt so good. She thought sh
would just hang on a little while longer.

Jenny filled her life with love, but nothing coul
take the place of the exquisite bond between a ma
and a woman who found each other special. And sh

did find Jake special; she found him extraordinary. Like all people, he was flawed; but his flaws only made him human.

She guessed she was selfish. But she was going to seize the moment, and then put him out of her life.

He kissed her until kissing wasn't enough—for either of them. She slid her hands down his back and tugged at his shirt. Underneath, his skin was hard and smooth and warm. He worked her skirt upward until he could put his hand on the soft smooth skin between her garter belt and her hose.

"Sarah . . . you bewitch me."

"Jake . . ."

Neither of them was capable of stopping. Jake worked the buttons of her blouse loose. She pulled him close as he explored her with his hands and mouth.

It was almost as if she had become someone else, as if she were standing in awe, watching another Sarah steal love with a dark and forbidden man. She knew she should stop, *had* to stop. Soon. But not now.

Sarah let her emotions run free. With Jake's mouth upon her she was floating, soaring through the hot summer sunshine that poured through the window. Her shop became a thing of beauty, a paradise created especially for this man and this moment. Mercifully the shop bell didn't tinkle, for Sarah was incapable of stopping what she was doing.

Sounds filtered through her consciousness, sounds that seemed to come from far off. Finally she realized they were coming from her. She was murmuring Jake's name, over and over.

The sweet torment of wanting him was so sharp she arched against him, calling out to him. Slowly he lifted his head and looked at her.

"Sarah."

She didn't want to leave her dreamworld. Closing her eyes, she fought going back.

"What have I done?" Jake's agonized voice brought her quickly back to reality.

He closed her blouse and began to fasten her buttons. "I'm sorry, Sarah. I didn't mean for this to happen."

"Don't apologize . . . please." She pushed his hands away and angled her shoulders to block his vision. Her face burned. She wished the floor would open up and swallow her.

Why didn't he say something? Why didn't he move? He was standing so close, she could feel his body heat. She was burning up. It felt as if the sun had turned into a fireball and lodged itself in her body.

She bent over her buttons, letting her hair swing down to hide her face.

"Sarah . . . Please look at me." She kept her attention on her buttons. Jake reached for her. With a finger on her chin, he tipped her face toward his. "Somehow you've gotten into my heart, Sarah. Every time I see you I want to touch you, to hold you, to make love to you."

"It's the same with me." She gave him a brave smile. "Crazy, isn't it?"

"Crazy . . . and very sad. I can't keep doing this to you. There's no future for us."

"I know."

He caressed her cheek with the back of his hand. His face was haunted.

"When I hear your name, I go crazy inside," he said.

"You should live with a dog named Jake." Her smile got shaky. "Every time Jenny calls the puppy I think of that wonderful day you gave it to her."

"How's Jenny?"

"She's napping right now. . . .She misses you."

"I'll come back . . . to see her."

"Yes, to see Jenny. But not"—she paused, waving her hand helplessly in the air— "this, Jake. Not this emotional roller coaster."

"I won't touch you again." He gave her a rueful smile. "If you promise to quit sending me money."

"Is this blackmail?"

"Whatever works for us."

Sarah smoothed her skirt and fussed with her hair. "You win," she said finally. "No more money."

They faced each other, the passion still fresh between them.

"I should be going."

"I suppose."

He gazed around the shop. "You've done a good job here, Sarah."

"Thank you."

Still, he didn't leave. In spite of everything, Sarah didn't want him to.

"Would you like to say hello to Jenny?"

"Could I?"

"Yes. It's time for me to wake her from her nap."

"I'll wait here."

Sarah left him standing in her Dollhouse. When she was out of sight, she leaned her head against the wall. How could all her good intentions have gone so wrong? She had let Jake come into her life all for the sake of Jenny. Had she been fooling herself about her reasons all along?

She straightened up and marched down the hall to get Jenny. It didn't matter what her reasons were. It didn't matter what had happened. Fate had decreed her life. There was no changing fate.

Jake paced the Dollhouse as he waited for Jenny. Desire was still tightly coiled inside him. Until he had come back, he hadn't realized the full extent of Sarah's hold on him. Not only was she in his mind; she was firmly entrenched in his heart.

And he was out of control with her. Being out of control scared him. He believed that as long as he kept tight control of himself and of everything around him, nothing bad could happen.

He braced himself, waiting for Sarah to return. This time he would maintain control.

The door opened and Jenny propelled herself across the room and hugged his knees.

" 'ake! 'ake!" she screamed.

"Hello, Jenny." He squatted beside her and took her in his arms. "I'm glad to see you too." Over the top of Jenny's head, he caught Sarah's gaze.

Jenny leaned back and patted Jake's face. "Play me, 'ake?"

"She's asking if you will play with her," Sarah said. "I'll tell her you're too busy."

"No. I'm not too busy for Jenny." He couldn't read Sarah's expression. "Yes, Jenny," he told the little girl. "I'll play with you."

"Good, good, good."

"Her favorite spot is the swing," Sarah told him.

"Then I'll take her there." He lifted Jenny up and started toward the door. "Are you coming, Sarah?"

"No. I'll stay in the Dollhouse. Please bring her back inside when you get ready to leave."

Jake carried Jenny outside and sat beside her on the swing.

"Go high," she commanded.

He set the swing in motion. Jenny squealed with delight.

"Go high, go high," she chanted.

Jake kept the swing going, and Jenny's laughter blended with the summer breeze. His heart contracted. He remembered another child, another summer, other laughter. Suddenly it seemed to him that his life was very sad. Fate had taken his child, and in closing himself off from agony, he had also closed himself off to joy. Hearing Jenny's laughter, seeing her little face turned up to his with love and trust, he wondered if he had made the right decision. Was love worth any risk?

As the swing rocked back and forth on the porch, Jake swung his gaze toward the window of the Dollhouse. He could see Sarah's silhouette. She looked beautiful and fragile and unreachable. It seemed appropriate to him that he was seeing her behind glass.

He stared through the window, transfixed with longing. Sarah looked up and caught his gaze. Her hand touched her lips, then she turned away.

Lonesomeness descended on Jake in waves. Even with Jenny at his side, he felt as if he were cast into the midst of a dark and stormy sea, the only human being left alive on the planet.

" 'ake?" He felt a small hand nestle into his. Jenny was staring up at him, her little brow furrowed with concern. " 'ake sad?"

"Yes, Jenny. I'm sad."

She leaned her head against him, and her voice was so ethereal that for a moment Jake wasn't certain he heard her correctly. But she kept repeating the phrase, over and over.

"Me love 'ake . . . me love 'ake . . . me love 'ake."

Jenny's words haunted him for days. She hadn't considered consequences at all when she had declared her love for him. She hadn't weighed whether she might be hurt or whether he might go away and not come back. She had merely followed her heart.

Was it innocence that allowed her to declare love so freely . . . or was it wisdom?

Jake stood at his bedroom window, gazing into the moonlit night. He felt trapped, trapped by a past that wouldn't let him go and by a love he dared not voice.

Me love 'ake. Me love 'ake. Jenny's words whispered through his mind.

The remembered warmth of her hand in his, tiny and trusting, stole into Jake's consciousness. Emotions he had stamped out and controlled for six years crowded in on him.

He allowed them to come. Alive with feeling, he imagined the future he had planned for himself, and he found that future intolerable.

He left his bedroom and went into his office downstairs. Without turning on the lights, he made his way to his desk and pulled open the center drawer. He found what he was looking for in the dark. Gripping the key in his hand, he went back up the stairs.

It was time to say good-bye to ghosts.

Nine

Jake slid the key into the lock and pushed open the bedroom door. Memories came back to him in a rush.

Look, Daddy. I can dance.

Daddy, Daddy. Will you make my clown come out of his box? He's broked.

I'm a cowboy, Daddy. Look!

Read my favorite story, Daddy. The one with the little girl living happy ever after with the three bears.

I love you best in all the world, Daddy.

Jake closed the door and stood in the dark. Bonnie's room smelled musty and unused. He had allowed no one inside for six years. Her toys were lined up on the shelves just as she had left them. In the moonlight their faces looked real. They stared at him, but their eyes were no longer accusing.

Jake waited for the gut-wrenching pain, the soul-blackening guilt. But neither came. Instead he felt the soft touch of memories too precious to forget.

He switched on the lights. Bonnie's crayons lay on

the table beside an open coloring book. Her favorite doll sat in the small rocking chair, its wax face fixed in a smile and its wedding gown turning yellow.

Daddy, can I be a bride?

Someday, sweetheart, when you grow to be a big girl.

Bonnie would never grow up to be a bride, but Jake no longer felt guilty. An accident had taken her life away, and he had let it take his as well. But no more.

Jake left the room, then came back armed with cleaning supplies. Far into the night he dusted and waxed and polished until Bonnie's room looked as if she had only recently slept there. Next he carted huge boxes up from the storage room. Then with great care, he packed away Bonnie's possessions—her books, her clothes, her toys, her jewelry.

Tears stung his eyes. But they were not tears of pain: they were tears of letting go.

By the time Jake finished his task, dawn colored the sky. He carried all the boxes downstairs and set them beside the front door. He would call the Children's Mansion to pick them up. Needy homeless children would play with Bonnie's dolls, wear her clothes, read her books—children he would never see.

Emotionally and physically exhausted, Jake stood in his hallway with the boxes. He felt purged—cleansed and ready to live once more.

Sarah and Jenny were in their backyard trying to catch fireflies. Jenny's laughter pealed through the summer dusk.

"You almost got it, Jenny. Try again." Sarah clapped and encouraged her daughter to snare a firefly with the net.

"Want light bug. Want light bug." Jenny swept the net through the air with such force, she landed on her bottom. Poking out her lip, she said, "Bad bug, bad bug."

"You can do it, Jenny. I know you can."

Jake stood in the shadows of evening, watching the two of them. No longer did he feel like a thief.

"Bad bug," Jenny said, arising majestically from her seat on the ground.

Jake's eyes crinkled at the corners with laughter as he admired her great dignity. She puckered her brow with concentration and set her mouth in determination. Across the way he could see the spark of courage in her bright blue eyes. For the first time since he had met her, he realized they weren't Bonnie's eyes at all. They were Jenny's eyes, the eyes of a very special child.

He moved silently across the yard, advancing slowly, savoring the sight of Sarah, unaware. She wore the filmy peach-color dress she had worn the first time he'd seen her in the backyard. Her hair was loose around her shoulders, blowing softly in the summer breeze. In profile he couldn't tell the shape of her lips, but he knew them from memory. And he wanted them . . . now and forever.

"May I join this party?" he asked.

Sarah whirled toward him, her hand over her heart.

"Oh, my." Her eyes grew wide, and for a moment she was speechless. Then she began the ritual he loved so well, smoothing down her dress and fussing with her hair. "I didn't see you."

"I didn't mean to frighten you, Sarah."

"You didn't frighten me. You can never frighten me, Jake."

"That's good." He smiled. There was so much he

wanted to say to her, so much he wanted to tell her. He shaped the words in his mind, just as he had done a dozen times on the way over to her house. *I love you, Sarah,* he would say. It was that simple. But standing beside her, drinking in her beauty, he found himself at a loss for words. Jake had never been at a loss for words in his life. He realized that he had never been in love before. With Michelle, marriage had been a necessity. With Sarah, marriage was a choice.

"Sarah . . ." That was a good start, he decided. Get her attention.

"Yes?" She smiled up at him, soft and sweet and pretty. Never before had he seen a woman through the eyes of love. His breath left him. So did his mind.

"Do you have another net?" he asked.

"Another net?"

"Yes. I'll help Jenny catch a firefly."

"Oh."

They stood staring at each other—Sarah with her mouth still shaped, and Jake aching to kiss her.

"Well, of course," she finally said. "I'll get it."

"I'll watch Jenny while you're gone."

She was a delicious ice-cream sherbet crossing the yard in her peach-color dress, a sweet summer treat that made his mouth water. And he had asked her for a butterfly net. Hell, he acted as if he had never *seen* a woman, let alone swept one off her feet. At the rate he was going, by the time he got around to asking Sarah to marry him, he'd be too old to consummate his vows.

"Dammit," he said.

"Dammit, dammit, dammit," Jenny chanted from the other side of the wildflower bed. Then she squealed with laughter.

Now he had done it. Not only would Sarah not

marry him; when she heard Jenny, she would kill him.

"Jenny, come here." He squatted down and she came loping into his arms. "How are you, sweetheart?" he asked, hugging her.

"Dammit, dammit, dammit," she said.

"That's not a good word for little girls to say."

Jenny puckered her forehead and cocked her head to one side. " 'hy?" she said.

"Why? Well, because it's a grown-up word."

" 'ake?" Jenny punched his chest.

"Yes, I said it, and I'm a grown-up." Jake was getting in deeper and deeper. How could he explain double standards to a child who had a hard time grasping the basics? It hit him with great clarity that if he didn't *use* double standards, he wouldn't have to explain them.

"Dammit," Jenny said staunchly.

Jake groaned. *Now what?* In the distance he heard the screen door slam. Sarah was coming. He took the easy way out.

"Sweetheart, don't use that word because your mother won't like it."

Jenny pinned him down with her knowing blue eyes. Then she arose from his lap and took up her butterfly net.

"Bad bug," she said, giggling. Then she walked away.

Sarah didn't go to Jake immediately, but lingered in the backyard watching him with her daughter. How tender he was with Jenny. How patient. Pangs of loneliness and regret squeezed her heart. No use dreaming impossible dreams.

She crossed the yard and handed Jake the net.

When he smiled at her, his eyes were so clear, she thought she could see his soul. For a moment Sarah was taken aback. Always with Jake there had been mysteries, darkness, withdrawal.

"Here you are," she said. "A net to catch fireflies."

"Thanks." He continued smiling, gazing down at her with eyes as vivid as green glass Christmas lights. She caught her breath. There was something lurking on the edges of Jake's mind, something important, something wonderful.

"Thank *you.* Jenny will love having a playmate."

"Good."

Still he stood beside her. *What?* Sarah's mind screamed. *What, Jake?*

Always when they met, he either held a part of himself back from her or got lost in the passion that seemed to overtake them so quickly. But this evening . . . She stared into his eyes, bewitched. This evening was different. A new person stared out from Jake's eyes.

"Well . . ." he finally said. "I guess I'll chase fireflies."

Sarah had to sit down when he left. Perched on one of Jenny's small chairs, she watched Jake cavort with her daughter. He looked the same as always—tall, vigorous, devilishly handsome.

Nothing is different. You're imagining things.

With a sigh Sarah put her dreams aside. What good would they do anyway?

The next morning Jake summoned his secretary.

"Gwendolyn, would you come in here?"

"You don't have to yell, Jake," she said, sashaying in. "That's what the intercom is for." She swung into her favorite chair, her hips encased in enough polyester to slipcover Texas.

"Do you mind telling me what you call that outfit you're wearing?" he said.

"I call it a bubble suit. Bert says when I'm finished with it, he wants the bloomers to use for a parachute." She leaned forward. "Now . . . do you mind telling me about that scowl you're wearing."

"It's not new."

"I know. Don't you think it's time to take it off and get it pressed or something?"

Jake stood up and began to pace. Accustomed to such behavior, Gwendolyn sat patiently in her chair.

Jake stared out the window awhile, reliving the evening with Sarah and Jenny. Abruptly he turned to Gwendolyn.

"Do I look like the kind of man a woman would turn down?"

"Turn down for what? Tennis? Volleyball?"

"Marriage."

To her credit, Gwendolyn didn't appear shocked. She laid her steno pad aside.

"I guess you and Sarah patched things up."

"Not exactly."

"You're telling me you proposed marriage to a woman you didn't patch things up with and she turned you down flat?"

"Not exactly."

"This suspense is making me old before my time. I'm going to resign." She stood up and reached for her pad.

"Wait." Jake pressed her back into the chair. "It's like this, Gwendolyn. . . ." He paused, remembering. How could he explain it to her?

Gwendolyn was patient longer than usual. Then she sniffed and shook off his hand.

"All I can say is this: If you were as tongue-tied with Sarah as you are with me, then it's no wonder she turned you down. She probably thought you were proposing a jaunt down the Tennessee River or a trek across the cotton patch."

"That's just it." Jake paced some more, all the while running his hands through his hair. "I didn't propose anything . . . exactly."

"How could she turn you down if you didn't propose?"

"I don't know. . . .We just kept talking about fireflies. We finally caught one for Jenny. Sarah put it in a jar. And then I left."

Gwendolyn stood up, smoothed the polyester over Texas, and put her hand on Jake's shoulder.

"Sit down," she said. When he was seated, she stood over him like a kindly dragon. "Now . . . what you need is a good lesson."

"A lesson?"

"Yes. I'll be Sarah and you propose."

"That's a wonderful idea, Gwendolyn." He grinned at her. "You won't tell anybody?"

"They can hog-tie me to a horse saddle and drag me through town naked. My lips are sealed." She sat back down in her chair. "Now, start."

"I want to marry you."

"Why?"

"Because I love you."

"Like hell, you do! The last time I went out with you, you brought me home and dumped me like a sack of potatoes."

"Sarah would never say anything like that."

"I don't know why not. No woman likes to be dumped."

"I didn't dump her. And besides, she would never

cuss." Jake glared at her. "You're not taking this seriously."

Gwendolyn laughed. "I'm trying to make it hard on you, Jake, because I believe Sarah is going to make it hard."

"She won't. She's a gentle, sweet woman."

"A woman rejected by two men . . . her husband and then you." Gwendolyn became very serious. "It's not going to be easy. I want you to know that. Sarah Love is not Townsend Publishing. You can't just march up to her front door and request her hand and expect to receive it. It's going to take finesse, Jake."

Jake became thoughtful. Gwendolyn was right, of course. Winning Sarah's hand would not be easy. What reason had he given her to trust him? What reason had he given her to believe anything he said? As usual, he had acted on impulse. He'd arrived at her house unannounced and unprepared. How had he expected anything except failure?

"I guess I'm not very good at love, Gwendolyn." He stood up, feeling as frustrated as a toad at a peacock party.

Gwendolyn came around the desk and hugged him. "Call me a sentimental old fool, but I believe you have what it takes, Jake." Unashamed, she stood back and wiped moisture from her eyes. "Now . . . get out there and do some old-fashioned courting." She picked up her steno pad and headed for the door. Over her shoulder she said, "And don't call me for anything until ten o'clock. I'm going to take a long coffee break."

"Why?" he asked, teasing her, giving her the opportunity to have a last biting word.

"Because I deserve it, you slave driver."

She flounced out, and he sat at his desk smiling. He had a courtship to plan.

Sarah's shop phone rang at four o'clock.

"The Dollhouse," she said.

"Hello, Sarah."

Jake's voice sent shivers over her. She clutched the phone to her chest a moment and breathed deeply before she replied.

"Jake, what an unexpected pleasure." Her heart raced. "You called about Jenny, I suppose. She was so glad to see you last night. She still has the firefly in her jar. Of course I'll have to convince her to release the poor bug, but—"

"Sarah . . ."

"What?"

"I didn't call about Jenny."

She sank into her chair and leaned her head on one hand. Out of the corner of her eye, she watched her daughter, her head bent over her sketch pad, humming and drawing.

"I called about you, Sarah," Jake said.

Her hopes soared. Then reality brought them crashing back to the floor.

"Do you need a doll?"

Jake's chuckle was low and sexy. Sarah crossed her legs and tugged at her skirt.

"That's a leading question, Sarah."

"Oh . . . I didn't mean to imply . . ."

"Dear Sarah." Jake's voice was exquisitely tender. "You're not capable of ulterior motives."

She wasn't so sure about that. Right now she was planning how it would be if she said "Jenny needs you." Jake would come, and she would see him in her Dollhouse, looking impossibly handsome. And he might kiss her, and she might kiss him back, just for a little while, just to ease the loneliness a little. And then he would say . . .

"Sarah, are you still there?"

She jumped, nearly dropping the receiver. "Yes?"

"I need to see *you*, Sarah." She held the receiver, waiting. "I need to talk to you. Alone."

"Tonight, after Jenny goes to bed . . ."

"Good. I'll see you tonight, Sarah. Until then, take care."

She wasn't even capable of saying good-bye. She was hardly capable of breathing. She held on to the receiver long after Jake had hung up. Her mind was whirling with questions. What could he possibly have to say to her that he couldn't say in front of Jenny? What would they possibly do . . . alone. The last time they had been left alone, she knew what had happened. Sarah felt warm inside, just remembering.

She agonized over Jake until a customer came into her shop. Sarah was so grateful for the interruption, she practically fawned over the poor woman.

"Let me show you the dolls," she said, the coming night looming large in her mind.

Sarah changed dresses three times after Jenny went to bed. A body would have thought she was planning to entertain the president. Finally she chose a soft dress the color of spring leaves, then settled on her sofa to wait.

The knock came at nine o'clock. Sarah tucked her stray curl behind her ear and went to answer the door. Jake stood on her front porch, illuminated by the glare of the naked bulb. His eyes were clear and shining, and he carried a bouquet of violets.

"These flowers reminded me of you, Sarah," he said, holding them out with a smile that was almost shy.

Sarah took the violets and pressed her face to the petals. When men came calling with flowers, they were usually courting. It was the old-fashioned way.

Sarah, she chided herself. *Stop jumping to conclusions.*

"Won't you come in." She held the door wide. Jake's leg brushed against her skirt. Sarah felt weak. "Thank you for the flowers." Pretending nonchalance, she carried the flowers to a vase, then took her time arranging them, keeping her back to Jake. When she realized she couldn't keep her back to him the rest of the evening without arousing suspicion, she turned and smiled. "All they need is water. Excuse me a moment, please."

In the kitchen she leaned against the sink. Even though a wall separated them, she could *feel* Jake sitting on her sofa, feel his heat, his power. She never should have agreed to let him come.

"What am I going to do?" she whispered. Her only answer was the ticking of the kitchen clock.

Sarah ran water into the vase and carried it back to her den. Jake smiled when she entered the room.

"I love that dress, Sarah. It becomes you."

"Thank you." She sat on a chair across from Jake thinking she could gain some advantage by studying his face. What she gained was a case of jitters. The dark and brooding man she was accustomed to dealing with had vanished, and in his place was a man with a purpose. What if he wanted to talk about what had happened at his mansion? What if he wanted her to become his mistress?

She waited, watching his face.

"I want to touch you," he said. "I can never see you without wanting to touch you."

Still, he remained on the sofa. Not knowing what he was going to say next, not knowing how she would respond, Sarah thought it wise to listen.

"This afternoon, sitting in my office, I made myself a promise, Sarah. I will not let passion get in the way of reason."

"That sounds sensible." Stiff with tension, Sarah sat on the edge of her chair. She was so tired of being sensible. Every day and in every area of her life she had to make sensible decisions. Sometimes her heart rebelled. At that very moment it was in rebellion. "Oh, Jake," she wanted to tell him. "Let's not be sensible this evening."

But she didn't say any such thing. Her life and Jenny's depended on her good common sense.

Jake leaned forward, his face intense. "Once I told you we didn't have a future together." She nodded. "I was wrong."

"What did you say?"

"I said, I was wrong, Sarah. From the first day we met, our future was sealed."

"That sounds like a fairy tale, Jake." Sarah struggled for composure.

"I kept coming back, telling myself I was coming to see Jenny, telling myself I was coming to repair your steps and mow your yard." He started to get up, then changed his mind and sat back down. "None of that was true, Sarah; I came to see you. I would drive by your house hoping to get a glimpse of your face or even the hem of your skirt."

"Please, Jake . . ." She held up her hand as if she were warding him off. "You don't have to say these things just to make me feel better." She paused for breath, then rushed on before she could change her mind. "I know you said you would leave soon, as soon as Jenny is back in school; but I want you to know that it's okay if you leave now. We can manage. We always have."

"Sarah, sweet Sarah." Jake left the sofa and knelt at her feet. He lifted her left hand to his lips for a warm, lingering kiss. "I'm not saying good-bye, my love; I'm saying hello."

Her hand trembled in his, but she didn't pull away.

"I love you, Sarah. I've loved you for a very long time."

Her hopes and dreams blended together in perfect harmony, and for a moment Sarah imagined a future with Jake. It would be beautiful, wonderful . . . and perfectly impossible.

"Please don't say any more, Jake."

"I must."

He pulled a small box from his pocket and snapped open the lid. A perfect heart-shaped diamond lay against the velvet. Sarah couldn't resist touching it. With one finger she traced the shape of the stone.

"Do you like it?"

"Oh, Jake, I love it."

"I thought you would." He pulled the ring from the box. The stone caught the lamplight and sent showers of sparkles across Sarah's dress. "I want to marry you, Sarah. I want to love and cherish you for the rest of our lives."

"What about Jenny?"

"I love her. She will be *our* daughter, Sarah."

All the love Sarah felt for Jake shone in her face as she gazed at him. How tempting he was. How easy it would be to say yes, to forget about the day-to-day problems of her life and pretend she could live happily ever after.

"No, Jake," she finally said.

"I know this is sudden, Sarah. If you want to think about it awhile . . ."

"I could think about it from now until the end of time, and my answer would still be the same." She stood up, out of his reach. "I will not marry you."

"Don't you love me, Sarah?" He stood up, ramming the ring into his pocket.

"This has nothing to do with love."

"It has everything to do with love." He caught her shoulders and pulled her against his chest. "Tell me you don't love me. Say you don't love me, can never love me, and then I'll accept no for an answer."

In the safe haven of his arms, regret sliced through her. And loneliness so great, she thought she would cry. She allowed herself to stay in his arms a moment, dreaming impossible dreams; then she pulled away.

"I won't tell you that, Jake," she said, facing him. "But I will tell you this: Bobby Wayne pledged undying love and then left at the first sign of trouble."

"I'm not Bobby Wayne."

"Maybe you're not Bobby Wayne, but I'm the same Sarah. I survived his leaving, Jake, but I could never survive yours."

Jake didn't reply immediately, but paced her room. His expression tore at her heart. He was fierce and yet vulnerable, determined and somewhat shy, extraordinarily proud and somehow willing to be humble. He was no ordinary man, and his passion was no ordinary passion.

Sarah fought against being caught up. She was tempted, so very tempted, but she didn't back down. Her future and Jenny's were at stake. She couldn't afford to be weak.

When he faced her, she could see his struggle for control. His hands were shoved deeply into his pockets, and the muscles across his shoulders were bunched with tension.

"I'm not accustomed to love, Sarah. I'm accustomed to casual affairs that demand nothing of me except my attention for a few hours at a time."

"Please don't say any more, Jake."

"I must."

"My answer won't change."

"Neither will my love." He reached for her, then pulled back without touching her. She was grateful, for she knew she could never resist his touch. "What I'm telling you, Sarah, is that I'm accustomed to taking whatever comfort I can get, and then retreating to my black moods and foolhardy ways."

"The motorcycle?"

"Yes, and the skydiving and any other damn-fool way I could think of to tempt fate."

"Because of Bonnie?"

"Yes." He came to her then. A shiver passed through her as he took her hand. He didn't lift it to his lips, didn't press it between his. Instead, he lifted it to the light and studied each finger, caressed each blue vein that crisscrossed her palm, touched the pulse point on her wrist. "I've held myself back from you because of what happened that night in the storm. Because of Michelle . . . and Bonnie."

"Don't. . . ." She pressed her free hand over his lips.

He kissed her fingertips, and she drew her hands away from him and clenched them behind her back. The need to believe in his vision of love and marriage made her tremble inside.

"Don't," she whispered again, for she didn't trust herself to say more.

"I'm free, Sarah. That's what I wanted to tell you when I came to your backyard last night."

"The fireflies," she said softly.

"Yes." He smiled ruefully. "I wanted to tell you that I love you and that I've put the past behind and that I want to spend the rest of my life with you and Jenny. . . .All I did was end up helping you catch a firefly."

His gaze was so direct, so sincere, she couldn't pull away. She saw passion in his eyes . . . and need . . . and love.

"I want you, Sarah," he said. "I want to love you and cherish you and protect you. I want you to lean on me and to hold me and to love me back."

She felt the tears gather in her throat. She swallowed hard and fought to hold them at bay.

"I can't," she finally said.

"Can't or won't?"

"It doesn't matter." She walked quickly to the window and stood looking out at the summer night. Behind her he was very still. What was he thinking? What was he doing? She dared not turn around.

"It matters, Sarah."

He came up behind her and turned her gently around. With the back of his hand he tipped her chin up so he could see her face.

"I won't give up, you know."

"I won't give in."

He gazed at her for a long time. Tension coiled through her until she could hardly breathe. His eyes changed as he leaned toward her. Her heart slammed against her chest. Without a word he kissed her.

She didn't try to fight anymore. She needed his kiss, needed his touch. When Jake touched her, her loneliness broke into tiny pieces and fluttered like small butterflies to some faraway place.

She wound her arms around his neck and pressed herself close. He felt solid and good. She wanted to lean on him forever, to give up the small day-to-day trials of her life and depend on Jake to take care of her.

His lips moved over hers with gentle insistence. Sarah let herself love him. Just for a little while.

His hands were strong on her, his lips gentle. Feelings poured through her like hot honey.

"Jake," she murmured. "Jake." Not even aware she had spoken his name.

He pulled her close, kissing her as if it had been invented just for the two of them. He kissed her until reason vanished. Nothing remained except need and desire and the two of them, standing next to the window, holding on to each other.

Take me, her mind screamed. *Take me into my bedroom painted blue and put an end to this exquisite agony.*

As if he read her mind, Jake broke the kiss and gazed down at her.

"Don't think I don't want you, Sarah. Don't think I don't want to take you into that blue bedroom and spread you across the bed and make love to you until you are too weak to say anything except yes."

She pressed her hand over her lips, saying nothing.

"I took advantage of you once," he said. "I'll never do it again."

He rammed his hand into his pocket and came back with the ring. The diamond caught the lamplight and threw sparkles across the front of her dress. She felt branded. For as long as she lived she would always wear his mark, would always carry the brand of his body against hers.

"This is yours, Sarah. I'll keep coming back until you agree to wear it on your finger."

Her throat was so clogged, she couldn't speak. Jake

gave her one last penetrating look, then walked out her door. She pressed her face to the window to watch him leave. He looked tall and strong in the moonlight, tall and strong and wonderful. And she wanted him more than she had ever wanted anyone or anything in her life.

At the gate Jake turned and gazed back at the house. The moonlight made his face look like a carving.

Sarah didn't move away from the window. Her last glimpse of him was too precious to miss. She would hold it forever next to her heart.

At last he turned and went through the gate. She watched until his car disappeared into the night. The tears that had threatened all evening rolled down her cheeks. She loved Jake . . . loved him enough to let him go.

With quiet dignity and resolution she picked up her telephone. Although the number was long distance and she could ill afford the cost, she dialed anyway. Desperate circumstances called for desperate measures.

Her old friend answered on the first ring.

"Jane, I know it's late, but I need a favor."

"You name it, you got it. After what you did for me, I'd walk on water if you asked me to."

"What I'm going to ask is much simpler than that."

Sarah spent the next five minutes telling Jane what she wanted. Later, as she lay in bed staring in the dark, she told herself she was doing the right thing.

Ten

Jake was not deterred by his second failure with Sarah. Eventually he would win her, and she was worth any effort, worth any cost, worth any wait.

The morning after his ill-fated proposal, he arrived at Townsend Publishing whistling.

"She must have said yes." Gwendolyn followed him into his office, determined to find out every detail.

"She said no."

"Then why are you so all-fired cheerful?"

"Because sooner or later she'll say yes." He sat down behind his desk, smiling. "I'm in love, Gwendolyn."

"Any jackass can see that." She snorted, but Jake wasn't fooled. Gwendolyn cared. She poured two cups of coffee and handed him one. "I guess all that practicing was a waste of my valuable time."

"I've found out that love is not a game. All the scheming in the world is not going to make it work."

She suppressed a grin. "What will, pray tell? An act of Congress?"

"Two, Gwendolyn."

"Two what?" She held up her hand. "No, don't tell me. Let me guess. Two fat wizards coming up with a secret formula. Two fat senators with nothing better to do but make it a law: Love must be reciprocated."

"Ahhh, Gwendolyn. Nothing can mar my mood today." He spun his chair and gazed out the window. "Did you ever see such a beautiful day? Did you ever notice how blue the sky is this time of year? How the trees look as if they're painted against a giant canvas?" He spun back around. "Until yesterday morning I didn't know birds had so many different songs."

"I'm going to be squalling here in a minute. I guess I'm turning into a sentimental old fool." She dabbed at her eyes with the back of her hand, then glared at him. "But don't you go telling Bert."

"I wouldn't dream of such a thing."

Jake picked up the phone and dialed Sarah's number. It rang seven times before he gave up. "She must be outside with Jenny."

An hour later he tried again. Still no answer.

"She must be doing some shopping."

He waited two hours before trying once more. The phone rang twelve times before he gave up.

"Gwendolyn," he called as he hurried past her desk, "I'm going out to Sarah's. I'll be back shortly."

"What about . . ."

He didn't wait to hear the rest of her comment. He didn't care if he had appointments with the President of the United States and the Prince of Wales to boot. He had to see about Sarah.

There was no sign of life at Sarah's house. He rang the bell and knocked on the door. No one came. He walked to the west entrance and peered through the picture window. The Dollhouse was empty.

By now, Jake was getting worried. Had Jenny had an accident? Had Sarah? What if she had fallen trying to do some damned repair to her sagging house and an ambulance had come to take her away? He passed a hand over his sweating face. So many bad things could happen to a woman alone.

Forcing himself under control, he walked to his car and drove back to Townsend Publishing. He was being paranoid. He was letting his past influence his thinking.

Sarah could be doing all sorts of errands that took most of the day. Or she could be out with friends. Hell, just because he loved her didn't mean he knew all there was to know about her. She probably had good friends in Birmingham, or even Florence by now, who had come up to take her on a little outing. Heaven knew, she deserved it.

He made himself settle into his work until evening. Sarah would be back by evening. Of that he was certain.

He waited until after eight to drive back to her house. When he saw the dark windows, he felt fear. What could have happened to her?

He rang the doorbell knowing no one was inside. He pounded on the door, knowing no one would come. He peered through the windows, knowing he wouldn't see a thing.

"She must be visiting overnight." The sound of his voice reassured him somehow. He even managed to work up a halfway decent whistle as he descended her porch steps. She would be back the next day. He had to believe that.

After a restless night Jake dressed and left for work two hours before his normal time. Sarah's house had the wilted unloved look of deserted property. Jake's chest got tight. He parked his car and went through her gate.

"She's probably not back from her visit yet," he told himself, even as instinct told him she hadn't gone on a visit. Something was terribly wrong. Sarah could be lying in her kitchen, dead from a fall from the kitchen stool, and Jenny could be walking through the woods with her dignified lurching gait, not knowing what had happened, knowing only that her mother needed help.

Jake jimmied the front door open and slipped inside. "Sarah," he called. His voice echoed in the empty house. "Sarah," he said, walking softly as if the sound of his footsteps might set off a horrible avalanche that would bury them all.

He wandered from room to room, calling their names. "Sarah . . . Jenny . . . Sarah. Are you here?"

In her bedroom he stood before the dresser. Her lipstick was there, and her hairbrush. He picked up the brush. A strand of her hair was tangled in the bristles. Carefully he worked the strand loose, then rubbed it between his fingers. It felt silky and alive. Need swelled in him, and love so great, he thought he would burst. And all over a single strand of Sarah's golden hair.

He took out his handkerchief and folded the hair inside. Then he put that part of her in the shirt pocket over his heart.

Next he walked to her closet. Her green dress hung there. So did the peach. He pressed his face against her abandoned dresses and inhaled the scent of her.

"Where are you, Sarah?" he whispered into the soft folds.

If he lost her, he would die. Fighting for control, he

took inventory of her closet. It seemed to him that a few clothes were missing—the pink shirt she had worn the day of the picnic, the skirt and blouse she had worn the day he'd found her in the Dollhouse, dancing.

He held on to the sides of her closet with his head bowed; then he went into Jenny's room. Her Pooh Bear and the set of books he had given her were missing. So was her box of paints.

He picked up a pink satin hair bow from her small dressing table. The memory of her laughter, high and bright in the summer evening, echoed through his mind. Gently he set the ribbon back in place and went into the den where the telephone was.

He called the hospital first. No one had heard of Sarah or Jenny Love. Next he called the police station.

"Missing persons," he said.

Fortunately for him, the man on duty was an old friend, Robert Ketchum. He listened to Jake's story without interruption.

"Jake," he said, when the story was finished, "take my advice. Settle down, go to work, and she'll show up in a day or so. She's probably just visiting friends."

"Probably so." After he hung up, Jake called the bus station. Had a blond-haired woman and a tiny special child bought two tickets to Birmingham? he wanted to know.

"Nope. Nobody by that description went to Birmingham."

"Russelville? Mobile? Anywhere in Alabama?"

"Nope."

"She's a beautiful woman. You couldn't have missed her. And she had a child, a little blond girl with a smile like an angel's." Jake was getting desperate.

"Did a woman such as that buy a bus ticket to anywhere?"

"Don't recall as she did. 'Course I don't stay at this winder twenny-four hours a day. You could ask Mike when he comes on shift."

"When would that be?"

"Two hours."

Jake called the small airport. He called the car rental agencies. He paced the floor, waiting to call Mike. He hadn't seen her either.

Sarah and her child had vanished off the face of the earth.

Jane Marks drove the car with careless ease, tapping her red fingernails on the wheel and humming. Sarah sat beside her, staring out the window. Jenny was on the backseat fast asleep, her puppy curled against her like a pretzel.

"Of course, it's none of my business," Jane said, taking the car north on the Natchez Trace Parkway, aiming it between the summer green trees and the red clay fields as if it were a missile set on a homing device. "But you never did tell me why you're running and where you want to run to."

"It doesn't matter why and it doesn't matter where. I just need a few days away from . . . to think."

"Well, naturally I'd take you anyhow, since you're the one who saved my marriage and my life as well." Jane raked her fingernails through the shock of black hair that always seemed to hang in her face. "Hell, if you hadn't gone through that drug rehab clinic with me, I would be somewhere in a plot of ground by now. And you taking care of Jenny, to boot." She reached for a cigarette and placed it, unlit, between her teeth. "I mean it, Sarah. I'll walk on water for you if I can, but I do think it might help you to talk."

Sarah shrugged her shoulders and kept her vigil at the car window. The trees blurred together, and she had the sensation of being caught in a tunnel with no way out.

"For one thing," Jane said, "you look like death eating crackers, and for another thing you let your phone ring and ring after I got to your house. And then last night at the motel you didn't eat a bite. Not one single solitary crumb."

Sarah reached for her friend's hand. "You deserve an explanation, Jane. And I promise I'll tell you everything . . . someday. But right now I need to get away from Florence for a little while and get my life back in order. Somehow I've let it get off course."

"You know I'll help you in any way. I'll wash the dishes, mop the floors, pay the bills. Hell, I'll even beat somebody up if you'll tell me who the culprit is."

"Just be my friend, Jane." Sarah squeezed her hand.

"You got it, kid."

The helicopter blades beat the hot air. Jake peered at the ribbon of highway below them, squinting his eyes against the glare.

"See anything yet?" Bert asked.

"Nothing."

"It's a wild-goose chase if you ask me, looking for a blue car that may or may not be headed north and that may or may not be carrying a woman and a small child."

"I know it's a slim chance, Bert, but it's all I have right now."

Bert adjusted his course, heading north from Florence. "I can just see you interrogating the neighbors. With that gloomy mug you probably scared that little old woman into saying she saw Sarah leave in a blue car."

"She was pretty certain."

"'Pretty certain.' Hell, when a woman says that, it means she has no more idea than a cat in a sack what's going on."

Jake squinted out the window, searching for a glimpse of blue on the network of roads.

"I see dust on that side road, Bert. Turn right."

Bert obediently turned the chopper. "We have a few more hours of daylight, and then we're heading in. Chances are Sarah will come back on her own." With his cigar clamped between his teeth, Bert turned to Jake. "She left her clothes behind, didn't she?"

"Yes. Most of them."

"There's no woman under the sun going to go off and leave her clothes. Mark my words, she'll be back. And you'll be sitting pretty, waiting for her."

"I can't wait."

Bert didn't bother to ask why. He just shook his head and kept the helicopter on course.

Jane turned the car off the Trace somewhere in Tennessee and headed east.

"Might as well change the scenery," she said.

Sarah just grunted. Jane gave her a worried look, then turned her attention back to the road. In the back of the car, Jenny slept on.

Soybeans parched from lack of rain and cotton stunted by the drought spread out in vistas along both sides of the road. Occasionally a few cows gathered at a pasture fence to watch the blue car as it whizzed by. Sarah let her mind drift. She was exhausted with being sensible and too confused for decisions.

"Is that a helicopter I hear?" Jane tilted her outside mirror and tried to see the sky. "Damned if I don't hear one. Funny . . . out here in the middle of nowhere."

"They're probably looking for some lost child."

"Or maybe an escaped convict. Gives me the shivers."

They drove on for a while, accompanied by the sound of the helicopter.

"Sarah, look behind us and see if you see another car."

Sarah looked. "No. Nothing."

"That's funny. I would swear that thing is following us."

"Nonsense. Just drive, Jane."

They passed three farmhouses, a feed store, and a wayside fruit stand. Still, the helicopter hovered near.

"They're after us," Jane said. "I know it."

Sarah rolled down the car window, stuck her head out, and peered upward. The helicopter had pulled ahead of them and was hovering, so close she could see two men inside. One of them seemed to be staring directly at her, and she had the uncanny feeling it was Jake.

"Nonsense," she said aloud, pulling her head back inside.

"Nonsense, what?"

"Nothing." Sarah clenched her hands together in her lap. She was getting paranoid.

"Are you in trouble, Sarah. Is somebody following you?"

"No. I'm not in trouble . . . at least, not the kind

you mean. And no, no one is following me . . . I hope. Keep driving, Jane."

"It's her," Jake said. "I know it's Sarah."

"Well, hot damn. A needle in a haystack, and we found it."

"Pull out, Bert, and land this damned thing. I've got to stop her."

Bert pulled ahead of the car and headed toward a pasture. "This is my kind of fun, Jake."

He set the chopper down, and Jake jumped out, ducking low under the blades. "Wait for me," he yelled back, his voice nearly lost in the noise.

The blue car was coming up fast. Jake had to intercept it. He sprinted across the pasture, his lungs burning with the effort. There was a fence between him and the road. He tore his pant leg getting across.

The car came around the bend just as he stepped onto the shoulder of the road. He could see Sarah, sitting in the front seat, looking pale but beautiful, her head held high, her chin jutting out with determination. Brave Sarah, taking on the world. Nothing had ever moved him as much as the sight of that delicate flowerlike face. His heart hammered so hard, he had to take huge gulps of air.

"Sarah!" he called, stepping into the road.

The blue car swerved around him, and for a desperate moment he thought he was losing her. Then he saw Sarah lean across the seat and grasp her companion's arm. Brakes squealed, and the car came to a stop in a cloud of dust.

Jake started forward, running. The car door opened and out stepped Sarah.

"Sarah!" he called, hardly daring to believe his luck.

She came toward him and they met in the middle of the gravel road. He reached for her, and she reached for him. Their hands touched, ever so softly, ever so briefly. Jake felt reborn.

"I thought I had lost you," he said, their hands hovering in the air like hummingbirds mating, barely touching.

"Oh, Jake." She drew her hand back.

Despair settled over Jake. She had run away from him. She didn't want to touch him. He fought against defeat.

"I have to talk to you, Sarah."

She fussed with her hair, causing a soft curl to come loose and curve around her cheek.

"It will do no good. My mind's made up."

Her eyes were very bright. He wondered if she had been crying.

"Please, Sarah. I can't let you go . . . not like this."

Sarah glanced back at the car, then up at him. Everything he hoped for, everything he dreamed of, was caught up in Sarah's blue eyes, shimmering and bright, waiting to burst forth, but holding back, holding back until Jake felt as if he might explode.

"Please, Sarah . . ." he whispered, loving her and wanting her and not knowing how to capture her without losing her. There were no guidebooks on love, no rules, no maps. Love was not a game. It was real, so real it made him ache.

The silence stretched between them, heavy with unspoken thoughts. Finally Sarah spoke.

"You deserve to know, but not in the middle of the road."

He took her elbow and guided her across the shoulder and onto a shaded turnaround. They stood together under an oak tree, her skirt brushing against his leg, his hand on her elbow, his fingers barely touching her blouse right under her bra line. Sarah closed her eyes a moment, dreaming; and then she straightened her shoulders and pulled out of his reach.

"If you came after me to ask me to marry you, my answer is still no."

"I've pushed you too hard. I realize that now. Just let me love you, Sarah. The rest can come later."

"No. It will never come. Not with me, Jake."

"Yes. Only with you." He couldn't stand not to be connected to her in some way. Very gently he pulled her into his arms and pressed her head against his shoulder. She sighed as if she had been waiting to settle her head over his heart. He caressed her hair. It felt silky and alive.

"I want romance, Sarah, and love and tenderness and kindness and laughter and joy. I want private jokes and cuddling by the fire and music that's special because I heard it with you. I want to protect you and cherish you and grow old with you."

Her heart accelerated. He could feel the increased rhythm against his chest. It gave him hope. He gentled her with his hands, allowing them to say all the things he didn't know how.

A light breeze stirred the oak leaves. Sarah lifted her head.

"I have Jenny." There was no tenderness in her voice, only a great and solemn dignity.

"I know you do. I want to have her too. I want to love her and help care for her."

She gazed up at him for the longest while, and he saw the fear moving in her blue eyes. He guessed the direction of her thoughts. A giant stone settled around his heart.

"It's not easy," she finally said.

"Nothing worth having is easy."

"You'll grow tired of the burden."

"She's not a burden, Sarah."

"Not to me. But eventually she would be to you."

"No. She's a joy. She will always be a joy to me, and very, very special."

"I can't divide my time, Jake. She needs me, and I won't let you settle for crumbs."

"Sarah . . . Sarah . . ." He cupped her face. "Don't you know now that with two, things work out easier. I can well afford a nanny, all the best teachers, all the very best care for Jenny."

"What about other children?"

Jake smiled, remembering Bonnie. "We will have lots of them, Sarah, beautiful little girls with your face and daredevil little boys with your bravery."

"Oh, Jake. Don't you see?" She walked away from him and hugged her arms around her torso. She kept her back to him as she gazed back toward the car, back toward Jenny. When she turned around, her shoulders were straight and her face was set.

"You're thinking of sturdy children who will play baseball and run with the track team and graduate at the head of the class and get married in white. You're thinking of *normal* children, Jake."

His heart seemed to stop. "Sarah . . . I know what you're thinking."

"No. No one can possibly know what I'm thinking, what it feels like to have failed, to be . . . flawed."

He caught her shoulders, forcing her to look at him. "The only thing flawed is your thinking, Sarah. Just because Jenny is special doesn't mean that—"

"Yes," Sarah interrupted him. "She's special, Jake, and I love her more than if she were the most normal child ever born." She clenched her hands into fists and pushed at his chest. "But I can't risk that again, not with anyone, and especially not with you."

"Then Jenny will be enough for us. If you don't want to take that risk, I'm happy to settle for having only one child."

"You say that now, but what about two years from now? Four years? Six years?" She worked herself out of his embrace and stood facing him. "I saw your face when you talked about Bonnie. I saw your love for her, your pride in her . . . your own flesh and blood, Jake, child of your heart, child of your loins. I won't deny you that."

The cold winds of despair blew across Jake's soul. Sarah was implacable. He made one last desperate bid to persuade her.

"I'll take all the risks, all the responsibility. I almost threw away love because of my past, Sarah. Don't throw it away because of what might happen in the future."

She reached toward him, and he thought he had won her. Her hand hovered in the air, almost touching his cheek, so close he could feel the heat of her, smell the perfume on her skin. He held his breath, waiting, hoping, praying. Then she drew back.

"No, Jake. I'm sorry." She turned to leave.

"Sarah, don't go."

"I must."

"I love you. I will always love you."

"Please, Jake . . ."

"Are you coming back?"

"In a few days."

"Permanently?"

"I don't know. I thought I could make a new life for Jenny and me in Florence. Now I don't know."

"I won't try to hold you . . . not now. But know this: When you come back, I'll be in Florence waiting for you. When you're ready for me, I'll be there, loving you."

"Good-bye, Jake."

"Until we meet again, Sarah."

He watched her go. Her back was straight and proud as she walked to the car. She never looked back. He stood under the oak tree until the blue car was only a speck in the distance, and then he went back to the helicopter.

"Well?" Bert said.

"She'll be back, just like you said." *And when she comes back, we'll work things out. There has to be a way.*

"I don't like to say 'I told you so,' but I told you so."

"You're a wise man, Bert, and a good friend."

"Where to?"

"Home."

Jane held her peace for ten minutes after Sarah got back in the car, which was a record for her. Finally she could stand the suspense no longer.

"Who was that gorgeous hunk chasing you in a helicopter?"

"Jake Townsend."

"That's all you're going to tell me . . . just his name?"

Just saying his name made Sarah ache. Talking about him would rip her into tiny pieces. And yet Jane had left her home and husband to take Sarah away on a whim. She deserved an explanation.

"I made the mistake of falling in love, Jane."

"What's so terrible about that?"

"He deserves more." Even as she said it, Sarah wondered if she were cheating herself as well as Jake.

Eleven

Soon after they left Jake, Jane and Sarah stopped for a picnic lunch on the side of the road. Jenny, finally awake in the backseat, was clamoring for food.

"There's no need to hurry now," Sarah said as she and Jane laid out the picnic on a quilt spread on a grassy knoll beside a small stream. "The problems I was running from have finally caught up with me."

"Your problems didn't catch up with you, Sarah. You never left them behind. They were there inside you all along." Jane peeled the brown crusts off her bread and tossed them out for the birds. "Believe me, I'm the world's greatest expert on trying to outdistance problems."

"Me 'ungry," Jenny said, making a sad face to go with her complaint.

Sarah handed Jenny a sandwich and a small plastic cup of milk, then turned back to her friend.

"What am I going to do, Jane?"

Jane chewed her sandwich awhile before answering. She was often flip and even scatterbrained, but when a real problem arose, she was equal to the task.

Sarah knew all that about her friend and waited patiently for her answer.

"I can't answer that. It's your life. Only you can find the right answer."

"I know that. Believe me, I do. But if it were you, what would you do?"

"Well . . . for one thing I'd get so damned tired of being wise and brave and sensible all the time that every now and then I'd do whatever I pleased just because it felt good." Jane peeled another crust off her bread and tossed it over her shoulder. Then she gave Sarah a shrewd look. "What feels good to you, Sarah?"

"Jake," Sarah said without hesitation. Then she blushed to recall just how good he had felt.

"See. You've answered your own question."

"I wish it were that simple."

"'ake?" Jenny tugged on Sarah's skirt. "'ake?"

"Here, darling. You can feed him." Sarah poured a small plastic dish full of dog food and handed it to her daughter. Jenny pushed it away.

"No. Big 'ake!" She turned her hands palm up and shrugged her shoulders in the eloquent gesture Sarah knew so well. "'ere?" She puckered her brows in a frown.

Sarah's throat felt tight. In sending Jake away, she had considered only one heart—her own. And now here was her daughter, puzzled and anxious and perhaps even suffering the pain of loss because somebody important to her was no longer a part of her life.

She scooped Jenny into her lap and hugged her close. Then she tried to explain their relationship to Jake in simple terms.

"Jake is at his house, Jenny. He lives in his house and we live in ours. You and I are a family, sweetheart.

Jake is not a part of our family. He's a friend. You can't always see your friends when you want to."

Jenny poked out her lips and punched Sarah's chest with one emphatic finger. Then she pointed to her own chest.

"That's right, Jenny. We are a family. Just the two of us."

Jenny pondered that awhile, then got off Sarah's lap and picked up her sketch pad and crayons. Knowing she loved to draw and could occupy herself for an hour at least, Sarah gave a sigh of relief. She hoped she had made Jenny understand.

"We've talked about nothing but my problems since you came to Florence, Jane. Tell me what's going on with you."

As the two old friends chatted Jenny's crayons scratched over the surface of her pad. She bent close to her work, occasionally frowning in concentration. All the skill she lacked in talking and walking and running was made up a hundredfold in her hands. They were gifted hands, swift and sure. Unlike other four-year-olds, who would do well to draw stick figures, Jenny drew people with recognizable faces. Art was her great compensatory talent, her gift from a gracious God who loved his special children best.

When she had finished her crayon drawing, Jenny presented it to Sarah. It was a picture of a house with a sagging front porch and Queen Anne's lace in the yard. In front of the house stood three people, holding hands—Sarah, Jenny, and Jake.

"Family," Jenny said, so clearly that Sarah was astonished. Then she punched her own chest. "Me love 'ake."

Sarah's hand shook as she studied the drawing. Summer memories tumbled through her mind— Jake riding the lawn mower while Jenny waved from the front porch; Jake eating gingerbread boys with-out heads and pretending that's the way he liked them; Jake singing Jenny to sleep and then carefully tucking her into bed; Jake sitting on the porch swing with Jenny at his side.

He hadn't had to speak his love; he had lived it. And she had been too blind to see. He said he wanted to love and protect and cherish her and Jenny, when, in fact, he had already done those things. All summer long he had been a part of their lives, steadfast and loyal and tender and protective. Totally unaware, she had already let him become a part of her family.

But she had been too stubborn to admit it. It took a special child to make her see the truth.

"Yes, Jenny. We are a family." She kissed her small daughter and held her close. Relief flooded through her, and feelings so exquisite, she thought she might fly into the sun and melt with happiness.

Jane stood up and began to pack the picnic sup-plies. "Does this mean what I think it means?" she asked.

"Yes, Jane. Take us home, please."

Jake stood at his window looking out into the night. Two days since he had tracked Sarah in the helicopter, two days since he had held her in his arms and she had told him the reasons she couldn't love him, wouldn't marry him.

He glanced over his shoulder at the telephone. It sat on his desk in his study, as silent and brooding as he felt. He left the window and picked up the phone. The dial tone sounded forlorn and impersonal. Was Sarah home? Was she still on the road?

He punched the first digit of her phone number before banging the receiver back into its cradle. He had pushed enough. She needed time. Yes, that was it. Time. Hadn't time finally made him see the truth?

He poured himself a glass of port, then stood staring into its depths. How could he endure the waiting?

His doorbell rang. Startled, he glanced at his watch. Nine o'clock. Who would be ringing his doorbell at nine o'clock in the evening?

Setting the glass aside, he hurried to his front door. His footsteps echoed in his big lonely house.

"Yes?" he said, swinging the door open.

Sarah stood on his doorstep. She was wearing the peach dress that made her skin look like delicate china. Her eyes were bright and her mouth was turned up in a smile of such radiance, Jake thought he must have somehow fallen asleep and been dreaming.

"Sarah?" His love for her filled him up, clouded his thinking, paralyzed his limbs.

"May I come in?"

He held the door wide. When she walked through, her fragrance seemed to saturate the pores of his skin. He drew that part of her into himself, holding on to it like a man hoarding his wealth.

She knew the way through his house. Jake followed her, flipping on lights. When they were in the great hall where they had danced together over the marble floors, Sarah reached for his hand.

"I need you to hold on to."

"Now and always, Sarah." Hope was reborn in him, and his house was filled with the light of love.

With her free hand, Sarah fussed at her hair. Her eyes were as bright as the wings of a bluebird. She squeezed his hand and smiled once more.

"This is hard for me, Jake."

"How can I make it easy?"

"By holding on and not letting go."

Jake folded her in his embrace. She pressed her head against his chest, and he buried his face in her hair.

"Jenny is home with my friend. Jane Marks. We've known each other since before Jenny was born. We were neighbors in Birmingham."

Talking about Jenny seemed to relax her. Jake held on, gently caressing her back. With Sarah in his house, in his arms once more, he wanted the night to go on forever.

"I called Jane when I . . . needed to get away." Her face buried in his shirtfront, Sarah kept talking. "I thought I had my life planned, an orderly life with Jenny. She's so very dear to me, Jake."

"She's dear to me as well."

"I know that." Sarah looked at him. "After you left in the helicopter, I was still trying to justify sending you away, still trying to think of reasons why I was right."

"And?" He smiled at her, daring to believe in a future.

"I was wrong . . . about everything. Over and over you have proved your love for me . . . and for Jenny. Heaven knows, you've had enough reason to walk away, but you kept coming back." She traced his eyebrows, his cheekbones, his lips, memorizing him with her fingertips. "I've come here tonight because I believe in your vision for the future."

Sarah's love lit the dark recesses of his soul, chasing away the last of the shadows that haunted him. With her, he was made whole. "The two of us, loving each other, will make it work, Sarah."

She backed away from him and caught his hand, smiling. "Have I ever told you I love you, Jake?"

"Never."

"Then I think it's high time to remedy that." She caught his face between her hands. "I love you, Jake Townsend."

"No woman has ever told me that."

"Truly?"

"Truly." His joy spilled over, and he laughed. "They've told me other things—what an expert at kissing I am and how well I dance and—"

"Shh." She put a finger over his lips. "From now on I'll do all the telling."

"From now on, Sarah?"

"Yes. Starting right now until we grow so old, you can't hear what I'm saying and my voice quivers when I say it." She pressed her lips full against his for a moment, then pulled back, radiant. "Jenny is the one who made me see the truth, Jake. She drew the three of us together as a family."

"A very special family, Sarah." He studied her. "Are you absolutely certain? No doubts?"

"None. My heart said yes to you long ago. It just took my stubborn mind longer."

"If I ask you a certain question one more time, what will your answer be?"

"Yes, Jake." She wound her arms around his neck. "Oh, yes. I'll marry you."

He swept her into his arms and started toward the staircase. With his foot on the bottom step, he gazed into her eyes. "This is need, Sarah, and desire and a passion that always gets out of control with you. . . . But most of all, this is love." He brushed his lips against her hair, down the side of her cheek, and across her lips. "I love you, Sarah."

"And I love you, Jake. Now and forever." She wove her hands into his hair and pulled him closer. "Let me show you how much."

"If I could fly up these stairs, I would."

"I'll be satisfied just to reach my destination."

The lighthearted playfulness he thought he had lost bubbled up in him. "And where would that be?"

"A certain bedroom of a certain dark-haired, green-eyed man who has no idea how very wonderful he is."

He captured her lips then, and held on to them all the way to his bedroom. When he crossed the threshold with her, he kicked the door shut.

"I hope Jane is prepared to stay with Jenny a long, long time."

"She won't leave until I return."

"You think she can hold out a hundred years with that little bit of food in your refrigerator?"

"How do you know what's in my refrigerator?"

They laughed together, heady with the discovery that love could be spontaneous and fun.

"I know almost everything about you, Sarah Love." He lowered her to the bed, then pinned her down with his hands on either side of her shoulders. Her hair was spread across his pillows, fair and bright. Her laughing lips tempted him. Her shining eyes teased him. Desire slammed him so suddenly and so hard, he almost lost his breath.

Seeing the change in his eyes, Sarah touched his cheek. "Jake?"

"The things I don't know, I'm planning to find out." He took her mouth in a slow and leisurely kiss. It was magic; it was miraculous; it was love.

"How long I've waited for this," he murmured.

"So have I."

He raised himself on his elbows. "I've dreamed of you here in this bed, your body next to mine, your lips . . ." He trailed his finger across her lips, gathering the sweet moisture on his fingertip. ". . . so perfect." He traced her ears, her cheekbones, the contour of her jaw. ". . . all of you . . . so beautiful."

"Hmmm . . ." She reached for him, whispering, "Love me, Jake."

"I plan to savor you." He began to unfasten the tiny pearl buttons on her dress. "The first time I saw you in this dress, I fell in love with you."

"When you stood beside that little table holding one yellow rose, I fell in love with you."

He eased the bodice over her shoulders. "Just the feel of your skirt brushing against my trouser leg was the most powerful aphrodisiac I've ever known."

"I wanted you to touch me."

"Like this?" He trailed his fingers across her throat and downward to the tops of her breasts.

"Yes," she whispered. "And like this." She traced a line from his chest to his groin.

Even with all his clothes on, Jake felt as if he were making love. He closed his eyes, savoring her touch.

"How have I ever lived without you, Sarah?" he asked, opening his eyes and gazing down at her.

"My world has been small without you, Jake . . . small and barren and without the greatest joy of all." She unhooked his belt and drew it from his pants. "The love between a man and a woman."

They undressed each other tenderly, marveling as if they had never seen the human body, exclaiming as if each part that came into view was a miracle. And when all their clothes lay on the floor, tangled together, with his pant legs wrapped around her skirt and her bodice trapping his shirt, Jake and Sarah came together at last, where they belonged, where they had always belonged.

Summer winds sang outside their window, and night birds serenaded the moon. Crickets and tree frogs and cicadas all joined the symphony.

Jake claimed his Sarah. He covered her, possessed her, and branded her his forever. And he learned one of the best-kept secrets of loving: That who you love is not nearly as important as who you are with the person you love. With Sarah he was a hero. She brought out every good quality he hadn't even known he had until she came along. With her, he was strong and brave and protective and tender and kind and passionate and true. With her he was reborn.

"Sarah . . . my darling . . . my love," he murmured, drowning himself in her exquisite body.

"Jake . . . my love . . . my hero," she whispered, welcoming him home.

The morning sun woke Sarah, its brightness pouring over her face, trying to get under her eyelids. She sat up, smiling and stretching, knowing she had slept late.

"Jake," she said, opening her eyes slowly. What she saw made her catch her breath. Violets were everywhere—spread across the bed, festooning the chairs, winking at her from the windowsills, nodding at her from the dressing table. She picked up a nosegay and pressed it against her cheeks.

"Good morning." Jake appeared in the doorway, carrying a tray filled with croissants and strawberries and cream in a silver cup.

"Is all this for me?" she asked, swinging her arm wide.

"For you. I plan to fill your life with flowers."

"You make me feel like a princess."

"You make me feel like a king."

He set the tray on the bedside table and leaned down to kiss her. "Are you hungry this morning?"

"Hmmm." She caught the back of his neck and eased her hands upward, through his hair. "Very."

"So am I . . ." He pressed her back against the blanket of violets. "For you."

"Just what I've always wanted for breakfast," Sarah teased. "Strawberries and you."

Breakfast lasted until noon. Then Jake drove Sarah home and went to his office.

Gwendolyn looked up from her desk, a comment hot on her tongue. When she saw his face, she broke into a smile that wouldn't quit.

"Good morning, Gwendolyn." He passed her by, whistling.

"Good morning, indeed!" She looked at her watch, followed him into his office, poured herself a cup of coffee, and spread herself into her favorite chair.

"Where's mine?" Jake asked.

"From that smug look on your face, I take it you don't need coffee to wake you up."

"You know I like my coffee first thing in the morning." He grinned.

"First thing in the morning." She snorted in her most undignified, unladylike way, then fixed him with a baleful glare. "In case you haven't noticed, it's nearly one o'clock."

"High time to start planning a wedding, don't you think?"

Gwendolyn was speechless for all of ten seconds, then she made a valiant comeback. "I want to be the maid of honor."

"If you promise not to wear that bubble suit."

"I plan to deck myself with a ribbon and come as Cupid."

"I plan to deck myself with joy and come as the groom."

They looked at each other a long time, old friends

who didn't need words to communicate. Gwendolyn
came around the desk and hugged him.

"I'm so happy for you, Jake."

"I knew you would be."

She gave him a final squeeze, then sat back down
and took up her steno pad. Jake watched her, smiling.

"Gwendolyn, do you think this company can survive if you take the next few days off to help Sarah get
ready for the wedding?"

"It will as long as you don't meddle with it."

She flounced out, and he sat at his desk laughing.
His life had taken a wonderful turn and was getting
better every day.

They had a garden wedding. Gwendolyn, gussied
up in a lavender dress the salesgirl declared made her
look twenty pounds lighter, bustled around the large
guest bedroom of Townsend Mansion, putting the
finishing touches on Sarah and Jenny.

"You look like two angels," she said, fluffing the
white organdy flounces of Jenny's dress.

"That's what Jake calls us. His angels." Sarah
adjusted her veil, then smoothed the folds of her
ivory satin gown. The salesgirl had argued with her
over the gown.

"It's not proper to wear white at a second wedding,"
she had said.

Sarah didn't worry about propriety. She didn't even
have to worry about being practical and sensible all
the time. Jake had not only given her love; he had
also given her a freedom she had never known.

She hugged herself. "I'm so happy I must be dreaming."

"While you're dreaming, dream off about twenty

pounds for me," Gwendolyn said. "It might make me fit this dress that old fool talked me into buying."

"Old fool," Jenny said, giggling.

Gwendolyn pretended horror. "Now I've done it. Jake will kill me."

"You should hear what *he* taught her to say." Sarah laughed. "On second thought, maybe not."

The sound of harp music floated up from the lawn. Sarah leaned her forehead against the window, looking down at the fairy-tale setting. Wedding guests sat in folding chairs under a white canopy. White carpet made a path between the guests to the minister. Violets in pots were banked everywhere. And waiting for her was Jake, a single yellow rose tucked into his lapel. Jake, her husband-to-be, her true love, her hero.

She bent over her daughter. "It's time to go, Jenny."

"Go 'ake?"

"Yes, my darling. Go to Jake. We're about to become a family."

"Good, good, good," Jenny said, clapping her hands.

"I've got a bug in my eye," Gwendolyn said, dabbing away with her white handkerchief.

"As long as it's a bug of happiness." Smiling, Sarah lifted the hem of her wedding gown and started toward the stairs. Jake was waiting.

He strained his eyes for the first glimpse of her. He supposed he looked calm enough, all spit and polish in his tuxedo. But inside he was laughing at himself. There he was, nearly forty years old, and as nervous as if he were the first man on earth to get married. That's what he felt like, the first man on earth. Adam, waiting for his Eve.

He saw her—Sarah with her white dress and her

white veil. The moment she stepped outside, the sun kissed her, gilding her hair and cheeks, outlining her exquisite body in gold. She was an angel straight from heaven. His angel.

She came toward him, her gown whispering along the white carpet, her face radiant. He almost lost his breath looking at her. Soon she would be his, to love and protect and cherish forever. He waited for the old feelings to come, feelings of a dark interloper, stealing a treasure he had no right to. He waited and waited.

Harp music floated around him. Birds sang in the trees overhead. A ray of sunlight filtered through the branches and crowned his head. A benediction. Joy filled him.

He looked at Sarah and winked. Her lips were moving, without sound.

"My hero," she was saying.

And Jake knew he was.

Epilogue

Two years later

"You're going to wear the carpet out." Gwendolyn tugged Jake's arm as he passed by her chair. "Why don't you do like the rest of the men? Read a book. Have a cigar."

"I don't smoke, and I've read every book on the market." He sank into a chair beside her and raked his hands through his hair. "What if she's not all right? What if something happens to Sarah? What have I done, Gwendolyn?"

She patted his arm. "You've done what any normal red-blooded American male would do. You've driven me crazy."

He laughed, then gave her a sheepish look. "Am I that bad?"

"Worse. The next time you plan to have a baby, don't call me."

"You'd be jealous as hell if I didn't."

Dr. Reinhart appeared in the doorway of the hospital waiting room.

"Jake? She's ready. You can come back now."

He stood up to leave. Gwendolyn grabbed his hand. "Jake, good luck."

Sarah was waiting for him, her face shining with happiness and effort and sweat, her abdomen great with their child.

She held out her hand. "Jake."

He took it. "We're in this together, Sarah. We're a team, a family. Everything is going to be all right."

"I'm not worried." She smiled at him. "Are you?"

He had spent the last six weeks in an agony of worry. Fear for Sarah and his unborn child had so consumed him that Gwendolyn had threatened to bar him from his own office.

"No," he lied. "I'm not worried."

"As Jenny would say, good, good, good—oh." Sarah grimaced.

"Are you in pain?"

"No." If lying would protect the man she loved, Sarah was not above it. "But I think this baby is trying to tell us something."

As if some invisible prompter had cued him, Dr. Reinhart appeared right on schedule. He gently poked and prodded and peered.

"It's time," he announced.

Jake held Sarah's hand as she was wheeled into delivery. He held her hand and wiped her brow as she entered the final stages of labor. And he watched with awe and reverence as his child entered the world.

"It's a boy," Dr. Reinhart announced, holding the baby high. "A perfect baby boy."

"Another hero," Sarah said, clinging to Jake's hand.

The doctor handed the baby to Jake, who didn't try to disguise his tears. He wanted his son to know that it was all right for heroes to cry.

Thirty years later
Vanderbilt University

Sarah and Jake walked the Vanderbilt campus hand in hand. The newness of spring burst around them, trees with fresh green leaves, flowers pushing up from the soil, sprigs of grass trying to become a lush carpet.

The crowd around them hurried by, chattering and laughing. Graduation always brought with it a party atmosphere.

"That day when we stood on the dusty road beside the helicopter, did you ever think we'd come this far?" Sarah asked, tipping her face up to look at her husband.

"I never doubted it for a minute." Jake took her elbow and brought them to a halt. He wanted to spend some time enjoying the sight of his wife's face before they joined the crowd. Sarah had changed very little over the years. Her hair was still soft and golden, with a few gray strands giving it highlights. When she was anxious, she still tended to push at it, causing that same curl he'd loved for so many years to come loose and caress her cheek. Laugh lines fanned out from her blue eyes, and she still made a perfect heart shape with her mouth when she was surprised.

Sarah reached up and touched his face, smiling. "I'm glad you chased me until you caught me."

Jake chuckled. "I still do."

"That's because I let you."

"If we weren't in a public place . . ." Jake traced her lips with one finger, then cupped his hand to her cheek. "I love you as much today as I did the first time I ever saw you, standing by the side of that road with dust on your face."

"And you're still my hero."

They gazed at each other with so much love that a few people stopped to stare.

"We're stopping traffic," Sarah said, laughing.

"I guess that's because geriatric passion is rare."

"Speak for yourself, Jake Townsend. I'm still a spring chicken."

They joined hands and walked toward the green where folding chairs were set up for parents and friends of the graduates. Sarah and Jake had reserved seats near the front.

The graduates filed in to the sounds of trumpet fanfare, first the undergraduates, then the masters candidates, then the doctoral candidates.

"Do you see him?" Sarah said, craning her neck toward the medical-school graduates for a glimpse of her firstborn son.

Josh saw his mother and gave her a thumbs-up sign.

"No, but I see her," Jake said, craning his neck toward the law-school graduates for a glimpse of his second daughter.

Victoria saw her father and gave him a V-for-victory sign.

There was a scurrying sound, and William slid into the reserved seat beside his parents. "Sorry I'm late. Got caught in traffic." When he crinkled his father's green eyes and smiled with a masculine version of his mother's mouth, his parents would have forgiven him anything. Besides that, he was their lastborn, their late-in-life child who was a bonus of their passion.

The graduates took their seats, and the ceremonies began. At the back of the stage, sitting beside all the dignitaries in their black robes, was a woman dressed in white, her face as delicate as a flower.

The president of Vanderbilt University came to the podium. Gripping it with his large hands, he leaned over and favored the audience with a beneficent smile.

"Our graduation speaker today is a most unusual

woman, a portrait artist of renown who has painted everyone from the President of the United States to the Queen of England's dog. Born special, she has succeeded against all odds. Two of her siblings are graduating today, a brother in the school of medicine and a sister in the school of law. We think it most appropriate that our address be given today by Jenny Love-Townsend."

The audience rose to its feet as Jenny came toward the podium in her halting, dignified gait. Before she reached it, she lifted one hand, as graceful as a butterfly, and blew a kiss to her family.

Jake reached for Sarah's hand as Jenny stood before the microphone. Tears stung the backs of his eyes. Jenny, firstborn of Sarah's womb, firstborn of his heart.

Jenny leaned into the microphone. Her hair, shining in the sun, looked like a halo.

"My words are simple . . . and straight from the heart." Her voice rang clear and true in the spring morning. Amplified by the microphone, it soared across the green like the music of fairy harps and silver bells. Only the lilt and the occasional hesitation marked Jenny as special. "Claim success. Whatever success means to you, claim it. It's yours if you work hard and don't give up. It's yours if you set goals and finish them. And it's yours if you have the love of friends and family." She paused and smiled directly at Jake and Sarah and William. Then she scanned the crowd until she located Josh and Victoria. Each of them received a smile that only Jenny could give.

"Do take the time to love," Jenny said, her voice soft and compelling. "For without love, success is empty."

She sat down to thunderous applause. Sarah and Jake wiped away tears, and even the unflappable William dashed a bit of moisture from his eyes.

The president conferred degrees, and afterward there was such a crowd around Jenny that Sarah and Jake had to wait in line. Victoria and Josh separated themselves from the other black-robed graduates and made their way to join the family.

"It's your turn next, little brother," Victoria said, ruffling William's dark hair.

"Yeah, squirt," Josh added, giving his brother a friendly cuff on the arm. "You have some big foot steps to follow in."

William gave them his famous grin. "While you two are arguing in a dusty old courtroom and cutting open dead people, I'll be taking Jenny's advice."

"Claiming success?" Josh asked, teasing.

"No. Taking the time to love. I just have one problem.

"What's that? Tell your legal-eagle sister. Maybe can help you out."

"I don't know whether to start with that cute blonde over by the law-school building or that fox redhead waiting for me back home."

Brothers and sister joined in laughter with Jake and Sarah looking on, smiling.

"Are you proud of our children, Jake?" Sarah asked

"I'm proud of all of them . . . most of all Jenny."

They held hands while the crowd swirled around them and their children's laughter lifted like kites toward the blue sky.

"Mother . . ."

Jake and Sarah both turned at the sound of the musical, faraway voice. Jenny stood beside them in her filmy white Victorian dress. Her hair was caught back in a bow. For a moment Jake saw her as a child at her tea party in a weed-choked backyard in Florence, Alabama.

"Daddy . . ." She slid her hand into his. He caressed the slim, talented fingers.

"I love you best in all the world, Daddy," Jenny said

She and Sarah exchanged a secret, special smile

THE EDITOR'S CORNER

What a marvelously exciting time we'll have next month, when we celebrate LOVESWEPT's ninth anniversary! It was in May 1983 that the first LOVESWEPTs were published, and here we are, still going strong, still as committed as ever to bringing you only the best in category romances. Several of the authors who wrote books for us that first year have become *New York Times* bestselling authors, and many more are on the verge of achieving that prestigious distinction. We are proud to have played a part in their accomplishments, and we will continue to bring you the stars of today—and tomorrow. Of course, none of this would be possible without you, our readers, so we thank you very much for your continued support and loyalty.

We have plenty of great things in store for you throughout the next twelve months, but for now, let the celebration begin with May's lineup of six absolutely terrific LOVESWEPTs, each with a special anniversary message for you from the authors themselves.

Leading the list is Doris Parmett with **UNFINISHED BUSINESS**, LOVESWEPT #540. And there is definitely unfinished business between Jim Davis and Marybeth Wynston. He lit the fuse of her desire in college but never understood how much she wanted independence. Now, years later, fate plays matchmaker and brings them together once more when his father and her mother start dating. Doris's talent really shines in this delightful tale of love between two couples.

In **CHILD BRIDE**, LOVESWEPT #541, Suzanne Forster creates her toughest, sexiest renegade hero yet. Modern-day bounty hunter Chase Beaudine rides the Wyoming badlands and catches his prey with a lightning whip. He's ready for anything—except Annie Wells, who claims they were wedded to each other five years ago when he was in South America on a rescue mission. To make him believe her, Annie will use the most daring—and passionate—

moves. This story sizzles with Suzanne's brand of stunning sensuality.

Once more Mary Kay McComas serves up a romance filled with emotion and fun—**SWEET DREAMIN' BABY,** LOVESWEPT #542. In the small town where Bryce LaSalle lives, newcomers always arouse curiosity. But when Ellis Johnson arrives, she arouses more than that in him. He tells himself he only wants to protect and care for the beautiful stranger who's obviously in trouble, but he soon finds he can do nothing less than love her forever. With her inimitable style, Mary Kay will have you giggling, sighing, even shedding a tear as you read this sure-to-please romance.

Please give a rousing welcome to newcomer Susan Connell and her first LOVESWEPT, **GLORY GIRL,** #543. In this marvelous novel, Evan Jamieson doesn't realize that his reclusive next-door neighbor for the summer is model Holly Hamilton, the unwilling subject of a racy poster for Glory Girl products. Evan only knows she's a mysterious beauty in hiding, one he's determined to lure out into the open—and into his arms. This love story will bring out the romantic in all of you and have you looking forward to Susan's next LOVESWEPT.

Joyce Anglin, who won a Waldenbooks award for First Time Author in a series, returns to LOVESWEPT with **OLD DEVIL MOON,** #544. Serious, goal-oriented Kendra Davis doesn't know the first thing about having fun, until she goes on her first vacation in years and meets dashing Mac O'Conner. Then there's magic in the air as Mac shows Kendra that life is for the living . . . and lips are made for kissing. But could she believe that he'd want her forever? Welcome back, Joyce!

Rounding the lineup in a big way is **T.S., I LOVE YOU,** LOVESWEPT #545, by Theresa Gladden. This emotionally vivid story captures that indefinable quality that makes a LOVESWEPT romance truly special. Heroine T. S. Winslow never forgot the boy who rescued her when she was a teenage runaway, the boy who was her first love.

Now, sixteen years later, circumstances have brought them together again, but old sorrows have made Logan Hunter vow never to give his heart. Theresa handles this tender story beautifully!

Look for four spectacular books on sale this month from FANFARE. First, **THE GOLDEN BARBARIAN,** by best-selling author Iris Johansen—here at last is the long-awaited historical prequel to the LOVESWEPT romances created by Iris about the dazzling world of Sedikhan. A sweeping novel set against the savage splendor of the desert, this is a stunningly sensual tale of passion and love between a princess and a sheik, two of the "founders" of Sedikhan. *Romantic Times* calls **THE GOLDEN BARBARIAN** ". . . an exciting tale . . . The sizzling tension . . . is the stuff which leaves an indelible mark on the heart." *Rendezvous* described it as ". . . a remarkable story you won't want to miss."

Critically acclaimed author Gloria Goldreich will touch your heart with **MOTHERS,** a powerful, moving portrait of two couples whose lives become intertwined through surrogate motherhood. What an eloquent and poignant tale about family, friendship, love, and the promise of new life.

LUCKY'S LADY, by ever-popular LOVESWEPT author Tami Hoag, is now available in paperback and is a must read! Those of you who fell in love with Remy Doucet in **RESTLESS HEART** will lose your heart once more to his brother, for bad-boy Cajun Lucky Doucet is one rough and rugged man of the bayou. And when he takes elegant Serena Sheridan through a Louisiana swamp to find her grandfather, they generate what *Romantic Times* has described as "enough steam heat to fog up any reader's glasses."

Finally, immensely talented Susan Bowden delivers a thrilling historical romance in **TOUCHED BY THORNS.** When a high-born beauty determined to reclaim her heritage strikes a marriage bargain with a daring Irish soldier, she never expects to succumb to his love, a love that would deny the English crown, and a deadly conspiracy.

And you can get these four terrific books only from FANFARE, where you'll find the best in women's fiction.

Also on sale this month in the Doubleday hardcover edition is **INTIMATE STRANGERS** by Alexandra Thorne. In this gripping contemporary novel, Jade Howard will slip into a flame-colored dress—and awake in another time, in another woman's life, in her home . . . and with her husband. Thoroughly absorbing, absolutely riveting!

Happy reading!

With warmest wishes,

Nita Taublib

Nita Taublib
Associate Publisher
FANFARE and LOVESWEPT

THE GOLDEN BARBARIAN
by Iris Johansen

Here is the timeless story of love and adventure set among hills of gold, warring tribes and fabled kingdoms—the story of a fearless princess and a barbarian sheikh . . .

Flaunting the oppressive destiny decreed for her by the kingdom of Tamrovia, Princess Theresa Christina Rubinoff struck a sensual bargain with a handsome barbarian chieftain. She vowed to play his seductive game, surrendering herself to his will, all the while determined to fight for her independence in a land that considered women only as playthings.

Mysterious as the desert night, rich as Midas, Galen Ben Raschid swept Tess away to his palace in exotic Sedikhan, offering her freedom in exchange for the marriage that would join their kingdoms. A man surrounded by enemies, he would make her a slave to his passion in order to bind her to his side, little knowing that when he took the captivating princess as his bride, he would lose his heart. . . .

In the following excerpt, Tess and the sheikh, now married, are returning to Sedikhan.

When Galen left the campfire and strolled around the pool toward the tent, it was nearly ten o'clock. Surprised, he stopped in front of Tess. "I thought you would have gone to sleep by now."

She scrambled to her feet. "I was tired, but not sleepy."

"Did Said furnish you with everything you needed?"

"Everything but sociable company." She added tartly, "Which you and Sacha certainly didn't deny yourself."

Galen held the tent flap back, and she preceded him inside. He took off his burnoose and tossed it on the cushions of a low divan. "I've been away for almost two weeks. Kalim had much to tell me."

"You didn't look as if you were conducting state business."

He turned to stare at her with raised brows. "That sounded suspiciously shrewish and wifely."

She flushed. "No such thing. I was curious . . . well, and

bored." She frowned. "I would have joined you, but the mere mention of doing such a thing sent Said into a tizzy."

"Quite rightly."

"Why? When members of the Tamrovian court travel, the women aren't stuck away in a hot, stuffy tent."

"You found the tent displeasing?"

"No." She looked around the tent. A thick, beautifully patterned carpet stretched over the ground, and everywhere her gaze wandered were colorful silk cushions, intricately worked brass lanterns, bejeweled silver candlesticks. "I've seen rooms at the palace that weren't as luxuriously furnished as this. "She went back to the primary subject. "But I don't like being imprisoned here."

"I'll consider ways to make it more palatable."

"But I don't want to stay here. Can't I join you in the evening around the campfire? If the court does not—"

"The men of your court haven't been without a woman for four weeks," he interrupted bluntly. "And your Tamrovian courtiers are tame as day-old pups compared to my tribesmen."

Her eyes widened. "They would insult me?"

"No. You belong to me. They would offer no insult. But they would look at you and grow hard and know pain."

Her skin burned. "Your words are crude."

"The fact is crude, and you must understand it. I will not make my men suffer needlessly."

"You would rather have me suffer." She scowled. "I would think you'd try to teach your men to control their responses. After all, I'm not that comely."

He smiled faintly. "I thought we'd settled the matter of your comeliness last night."

She had not thought her cheeks could get any hotter, but she found she was wrong. "Not everyone would find me to their taste. I think you must be a little peculiar."

He chuckled, and his face looked as boyish as it had when he'd laughed and joked with his men. "I assure you that my tastes are not at all unusual. You have a quality I've seen in few women."

She gazed at him warily. "What?"

"Life." His eyes held her own, and his expression suddenly sobered. "I've never met a woman so alive as you, *kilen*."

Her stomach fluttered as she looked at him. She tore her gaze away from his face to stare down at the patterns in the carpet. "Your women are without spirit?"

"They have spirit," he said softly. "But they don't light up a tent by merely walking into it."

The flutter came again, and with it a strange breathlessness. "Pretty words. But what you're about to say is that I *must* stay in the tent."

"What I'm saying is that I prefer to save your light for myself."

Joy soared through her with bewildering intensity. She mustn't let him sway her feelings like this, she thought desperately. Sacha had said Galen gave whatever was demanded of him. Perhaps he thought this flattery was what she wanted of him. "As I said, pretty words." She changed the subject as she forced herself to lift her eyes to gaze directly at him. "You look different in your robe."

"More the barbarian?"

"I didn't say that," she said quickly.

"But you thought it." He smiled bitterly. "I've embraced many of your civilized Western ways, but I refuse to give up everything. The material of our robes is thin, comfortable, and the white reflects the sun." He strolled to the small trunk in the corner. "Which reminds me, you look most uncomfortably hot in your velvet riding habit. I think we must do something about it." He rummaged until he found another robe like the one he was wearing. "Here, put this on." He turned and tossed the garment to her. "You'll find it far more satisfactory."

"My habit is comfortable."

"And unattractive enough to satisfy me when you're out of the tent in the presence of my men." He met her gaze. "But not when we're alone. Put on the robe."

She was to dress herself to please him. She knew wives did such things, but the idea was somehow . . . intimate. The air between them changed, thickened. She was suddenly acutely conscious of the soft texture of the cotton robe in her hands, the sound of Said's flute weaving through the darkness, the intensity of Galen's expression as he gazed at her. She swallowed. "Very well." She began to undo the fastening at the throat of her brown habit.

He watched her for a minute before he turned and strode toward the entrance of the tent.

"You're leaving?" she asked, startled. "I thought—" She broke off, her tongue moistening her lower lip.

"You thought I would want to look at you again." He smiled. "I do. But it was easier last night at the inn, with all the trappings of civilization about me. Here, I'm freer and must take care." He lifted the flap of the tent, and the next moment she saw him standing outside, silhouetted by the moonlight against the vast dark sky.

He wasn't going to leave her. The rush of relief surging through her filled her with confusion and fear. Surely, the only reason she didn't want him to leave was because she had felt so alone in such a strange land, she assured herself. She couldn't really care if he went back to the tribesmen by the fire.

"*Dépêches-toi,*" he said softly, not looking at her.

Her hands flew, undoing the fastenings of the habit, and a few minutes after she was slipping naked into the softness of the robe.

It was far too large for her, the hem dragging the floor, the sleeves hanging ridiculously long. On her small frame the robe looked ludicrous and not at all seductive. She strode over to the trunk and rummaged until she found a black silk sash, wound the length three times around her waist, and tied it in a knot in front before before rolling up the sleeves to her elbows. The garment was so voluminous she should have felt uncomfortable, but the cotton was light as air compared to her habit. She ruffled her hair before stalking belligerently toward the opening of the tent. "I look foolish. You must promise not to laugh at me."

"Must I?" He continued to look at the campfire across the pond. "But laughter is so rare in this world."

"Well, I have no desire to provide you with more." She stopped beside him and scowled up at him. "I'm sure I don't look in the least what you intended. But it's your fault. I told you that I wasn't comely."

"So you did." His gaze shifted to her face and then down her draped body. His lips twitched. "You do look a trifle . . . overwhelmed." He sobered. "But you're wrong, it's exactly what I intended."

"Truly?" She frowned doubtfully. How could she be expected to gain understanding of the man when he changed from moment to moment? Last night he had wanted her without clothing, and now it appeared he desired her to be covered from chin to toes. She shrugged. "But you're right, this is much more comfortable than my habit."

"I'm glad you approve." His mouth turned up at the corners. "I should have hated to be proved wrong."

"You would never admit it. Men never do. My father—"

He frowned. "I find I'm weary of being compared to your father."

She could certainly understand his distaste. "I'm sorry," she said earnestly. I know few men, so perhaps I'm being unfair. I can see how you would object to being tossed in the same stable as my father, for he's not at all pleasant."

He started to smile, and then his lips thinned. "No, not at all pleasant." He reached out and touched her hair with a gentle hand. "But you don't have to worry about him any longer, *kilen*."

"I don't worry about him." She shrugged. "It would be a waste of time to worry about things I can't change. It's much more sensible to accept the bad and enjoy the good in life."

"Much more sensible." His fingers moved from her hair to brush the shadows beneath her eyes. "I drove us at a cruel pace from Dinar. Was the day hard for you?"

Her flesh seemed to tingle beneath his touch, filling her with the same excitement and panic she had known the night before. She had to force herself not to step away from him. "No, I would not admit to being so puny. I did not sleep well last night." She had not meant to blurt that out, she thought vexedly. "I mean—"

"I know what you mean. I did not sleep well either." Galen turned her around and shoved her gently toward the tent. "Which is why I pushed the pace today. I wanted to be weary enough to sleep tonight. Good night, *kilen*."

"Aren't you coming?"

"Presently. Go to bed."

She wanted to argue, but there was something about the tension of the back he turned toward her that gave her pause. Still, for some reason she hesitated, reluctant to leave him. "What time do we leave tomorrow?"

"At dawn."

"And how long will it take to get to Zalandan?"

"Another five days."

"Will we—"

"Go to bed, Tess!"

The suppressed violence in his voice made her jump and start hurriedly toward the entrance of the tent. "Oh, very well." She entered the tent and then slowed her pace to a deliberate stroll as she moved toward the curtained sleeping area. After all, there was nothing to run away from when Galen was not even in pursuit.

She drew back the thin curtain and the next moment sank onto the cushions heaped on the low, wide divan. There was much to say for barbarism, she thought as she burrowed into the silken pillows. This divan was much more comfortable than the bed at the inn. . . .

• • •

Tess's curly hair was garnet-dark flame against the beige satin of the pillow under her head. His robe had worked open revealing her delicate shoulder, the skin of which was soft as velvet and even more luminescent than the satin of the pillow below it.

As Galen watched, she stirred, half turned, and a beautifully formed limb emerged from the cotton folds of the robe. Not a voluptuous thigh but a strong, well-muscled one.

Exquisite. He felt a painful thickening in his groin as he stood looking at her. He had deliberately provided her with the oversized garment to avoid seeing her naked as he had last night, but somehow this half nudity was even more arousing.

It was because he was back in Sedikhan, he told himself. It couldn't be this half-woman, half-child who was causing his physical turmoil. He always felt a seething unrest and wildness when he was on home ground. The memories of his past debaucheries were to vivid to be ignored when he was back in the desert. But the wildness had never been this strong, the urge to take a woman so violent. . . .

But he could control it. He had to control it.

Why? She was only a woman, like any other.

No, not like any other. She had a man's sense of honor. She had made a bargain and would keep it. He could have her simply by reaching out a hand. He could put his palm on those soft, springy curls surrounding her womanhood and stroke her as he did Selik. He could pluck at that delicious secret nub until she screamed for satisfaction. He could pull her to her knees and make—

Make. The word cooled his fever for her. Only a true barbarian used force on women.

He stripped quickly, blew out the candle in the copper lantern hanging on the tent pole, and settled down on the cushions beside Tess, careful not to touch her. The heaviness in his loins turned painful. He lay with his back to her, his heart pounding against his rib cage.

He could control it. He was no savage to take—

He felt the cushions shift. The scent of lavender and woman drifted over him, and he tried to breathe shallowly to mitigate its effect.

Then he felt her fingers in his hair.

Every muscle in his body went rigid. "Tess?"

She murmured something drowsily, only half-awake, her fingers caressing his nape.

"What"—a shudder racked through him as her fingertips brushed his shoulders—"are you doing?"

She pulled the ribbon from his queue and tossed it aside. "Wife's duty . . ."

She moved away again, and the rhythm of her breathing told him she was sound asleep once more.

Wife's duty? Galen would have laughed if he hadn't been in the grip of hot frustration. He would like to show her a wife's "duty." He would like to move between her thighs and plunge deep. He would like to take her for a ride in the desert *coït de cheval*, cradling her buttocks in his palms, making her feel every inch of him. He would like to— He forced himself to abandon such thoughts and to unclench his fists.

He had put his wild days behind him. He could no longer take with reckless abandon. He must think, consider, wait.

Dear God in heaven, he was hurting.

LUCKY'S LADY
by Tami Hoag

As wild and mysterious as the Louisiana swamp he called home, Lucky Doucet was an infuriatingly attractive Cajun no woman could handle. He believed there was no room in his solitary life for the likes of elegant Serena Sheridan, but he couldn't deny her desperate need to find her missing grandfather. He would help her but nothing more—yet once he felt the lure of the flaxen-haired beauty, an adventurer like Lucky couldn't resist playing with fire for long.

Serena felt unnerved, aroused, and excited by the ruggedly sexy renegade whose gaze burned her with its heat, but did she dare tangle with a rebel whose intensity was overwhelming, who claimed his heart was a no-man's land?

In the following excerpt, Lucky is taking Serena to his house in the swamp . . . to spend the night.

"Me, I'd say there's a lotta things here you don' understand, sugar," Lucky drawled.

Not the least of which was *him*, Serena thought, plucking at the edge of the mosquito netting. The man was a jumble of contradictions. Mean to her one minute and throwing mosquito netting over her the next; telling her in one breath he didn't involve himself in other people's affairs, then giving his commentary on the situation. She wouldn't have credited him with an abundance of compassion, but he was rescuing her from having to spend the night outside, and, barring nefarious reasons, compassion was the only motive she could see.

She wondered what kind of place he was taking her to. She didn't hold out much hope for luxurious accommodations. Her idea of a poacher's lair was just a notch above a cave with animal hides scattered over the floor. She pictured a tar-paper shack and a mud yard littered with dead electricity generators and discarded butane tanks. There would probably be a tumbledown shed full of poaching paraphernalia, racks of stolen pelts and buckets of rancid muskrat remains. She couldn't imagine Lucky hanging curtains. He struck her as the sort of man who would pin up centerfolds from raunchy magazines on the walls and call it art.

They rounded a bend in the bayou, and a small, neat house came into view. It was set on a tiny hillock in an alcove that had been cleared of trees. Its weathered-cypress siding shimmered pale silver in the fading light. It was a house in the old Louisiana country style, an Acadian house built on masonry piers to keep it above the damp ground. Steps led onto a deep gallery that was punctuated by shuttered windows and a screen door. An exterior staircase led up from the gallery to the overhanging attic that formed the ceiling of the gallery—a classic characteristic of Cajun architecture. Slim wooden columns supporting the overhang gave the little house a gracious air.

Serena was delightfully surprised to see something so neat and civilized in the middle of such a wilderness, but nothing could have surprised her more than to hear Lucky tell her it was his.

He scowled at the look of utter shock she directed up at him through the mosquito netting. "What'sa matter, *chère?* You were expecting some old white-trash shack with a yard full of pigs and chickens rootin' through the garbage?"

"Stop putting words in my mouth," she grumbled, unwilling to admit her unflattering thoughts, no matter how obvious they might have been.

A corner of Lucky's mouth curled upward, and his heavy-lidded eyes focused on her lips with the intensity of lasers. "Is there something else you want me to put there?"

Serena's heart thudded traitorously at the involuntary images that flitted through her mind. It was all she could do to keep her gaze from straying to the part of his anatomy that was at her eye level.

"You've really cornered the market on arrogance, haven't you?" she said, as disgusted with herself as she was with him.

"Me?" he said innocently, tapping a fist to his chest. "*Non.* I just know what a woman really wants, that's all."

"I'm sure you don't have the vaguest idea what a woman really wants," Serena said as she untangled herself from the *baire* and tossed it aside. She offered Lucky her hand as if she were a queen, and allowed him to hand her up onto the dock, giving him a smug smile as her feet settled on the solid wood. "But if you want to go practice your theory on yourself, don't let me stop you."

Lucky watched her walk away, perversely amused by her sass. She was limping slightly, but that didn't detract from the alluring sway of the backside that filled her snug white pants to heart-shaped perfection. Desire coiled like a spring in his gut. He might not have known what Miss Sheridan really wanted, but he damn well knew what his body wanted.

It was going to be a long couple of days.

He pulled the pirogue up out of the water and left it with its cargo of suitcases and crawfish to join Serena on the gallery. He didn't like having her there. This place revealed things about him. Having her there allowed her to get too close when his defenses were demanding to keep her an emotional mile away. He might have wanted her physically, but that was as far as it went. He had learned the hard way not to let anyone inside the walls he had painstakingly built around himself. He would have been safer if she could have gone on believing he lived like an animal in some ancient rusted-out house trailer.

"It's very nice," she said politely as he trudged up the steps onto the gallery.

"It's just a house," he growled, jerking the screen door open. "Go in and sit down. I'm gonna take the sliver out of that foot of yours before gangrene sets in."

Serena bared her teeth at him a parody of a smile. "Such a gracious host," she said, sauntering in ahead of him.

The interior of the house was as much of a surprise to her as the exterior had been. It consisted of two large rooms, both visible from the entrance—a kitchen and dining area, and a bedroom and living area. The place was immaculate. There was no pile of old hunting boots, no stacks of old porno magazines, no mountains of laundry, no litter of food-encrusted pots and pans. From what Serena could see on her initial reconnaissance, there wasn't as much as a dust bunny on the floor.

Lucky struck a match and lit a pair of kerosene lamps on the dining table, flooding the room with buttery-soft light, then left the room without a word. Serena pulled out a chair and sat down, still marveling. His decorating style was austere, as spare and plain as an Amish home, a style that made the house itself seem like a work of art. The walls had a wainscoting of varnished cypress paneling beneath soft white plaster. The furnishings appeared to be meticulously restored antiques—a wide-plank cypress dining table, a large French armoire that stood against the wall, oak and hickory chairs with rawhide seats. In the kitchen area mysterious bunches of plants had been hung by their stems from a wide beam to dry. Ropes of garlic and peppers adorned the window above the sink in lieu of a curtain.

Lucky appeared to approve of refrigeration and running water, but not electric lights. Another contradiction. It made Serena vaguely uncomfortable to think there was so much more to him than she had been prepared to believe. It would have been easy to dislike a man who lived in a hovel and poached for a living. This house and its contents put him in a whole other light—one he didn't particularly like to have her see him in, if the look on his face was any indication.

He emerged with first aid supplies cradled in one brawny arm from what she assumed was a bathroom. These he set on the table, then he pulled up a chair facing hers and jerked her foot up onto his lap, nearly pulling her off her seat. He tossed her shoe aside and gave her bare foot a ferocious look, lifting it to eye level and turning it to capture the best light. Serena clutched the arm of her chair with one hand and the edge of the table with the other, straining against tipping over backward. She winced as Lucky prodded at the sliver.

"Stubborn as that grandpapa of yours, walkin' around half the day with this in your foot," he grumbled, playing the tweezers. *"Espèsces de tête dure."*

"What does that mean? Ouch!"

"You're a hardheaded thing."

"Ouch" She tried to jerk her foot back.

"Be still!"

"You sadist!"

"Quit squirming!"

"Ou-ou-ouch!"

"Got it."

She felt an instant of blessed relief as soon as the splinter was out of her foot, but it was short-lived. Serena hissed through her teeth at the first sting of the alcohol, blinking furiously at the tears that automatically rose in her eyes.

"Your bedside manner leaves a lot to be desired," she said harshly.

Lucky raised his eyes and stared at her over her toes. The corners of his mouth turned up. "Yeah, but my manner *in* bed won't leave anything to be desired. I can promise you that, *chère.*"

Serena met his hypnotic gaze, her heart beating a wild pulse in her throat as his long fingers gently traced the bones of her foot and ankle. All thoughts of pain vanished from her head. Desire coursed through her veins in a sudden hot stream that both excited and frightened her. She didn't react this way to men. She certainly shouldn't have been reacting his way to *this* man. Wha had become of her common sense? What had become of her control?

With an effort she found her voice, but it was soft and smoky and she barely recognized it when she spoke. "That's no promise, that's a threat."

Lucky eased her foot down and rose slowly. His fingers curled around the arms of Serena's chair and he tilted it back on its hind legs, his eyes never leaving hers as he leaned down close.

"Is it?" he said in a silken whisper, his mouth inches from hers. "Are you afraid of me, *chère?*"

"No," she said, the tremor in her voice making a mockery of her answer. She stared at him, eyes wide, her breath escaping in a thin stream from between her parted lips. The molten heat in his gaze stirred an answering warmth inside her and she found herself suddenly staring at his mouth, that incredibly sensuous, beautifully carved mouth.

"You're not afraid of me?" he said, arching a brow, the words barely audible. He leaned closer still. "Then mebbe this is what you're afraid of."

He closed the distance between them, touching his lips to hers.

The heat was instantaneous. It burst around them and inside them, as bright and hot as the flare of the lamps on the table beside them. Serena sucked in a little gasp, drawing Lucky closer. He settled his mouth against hers, telling himself he wanted just a taste of her, nothing more, but fire swept through him, his blood scalding his veins. One taste. Just one taste . . . would never be enough.

Her mouth was like silk soaked in wine—soft, sweet, intoxicating. His tongue slipped between her parted lips to better savor the experience. He stroked and explored and Serena responded in kind, reacting on instinct. Her tongue slid sinuously against Lucky's. His plunged deeper into her mouth. The flames leapt higher.

A moan drifted up from Serena's throat, and her arms slid up around Lucky's neck. She could feel herself growing dizzy, as if her body were floating up out of the chair. Dimly she realized Lucky was rising and pulling her up with him. His arms banded around her like steel, lifting her, pulling her close. His big hands slid down to the small of her back and pressed her into him.

He was fully aroused. His erection pressed into her belly, as hard as granite, as tempting as sin. She arched against it wantonly, reacting without thought. A growl rumbled deep in his chest, and he rolled his hips against her as he changed the angle of the kiss and plunged his tongue into her mouth again and again.

He stroked a hand down over the full swell of one hip. Cupping her buttock, he lifted her to bring her feminine mound up against his hardness. She made a small, frightened sound in her throat and need surged through him like a flood. He wanted her. God, he wanted her! He wanted to take her right here, right now, on the table, on the floor. It was madness.

Madness.

Sweet heaven, what was he doing? he wondered, finally hearing the alarm bells clanging in his head. What was she doing to him? He set her away from him with a violence that made her stumble back against the chair she'd been sitting in. She stared at him, her eyes wide and dark with a seductive mix of passion and fear. Her hair tumbled around her shoulders in golden disarray. Her mouth, swollen and red from the force of his kiss, trembled. She stared at him as if he were something wild and terrifying.

Wild was exactly what he was feeling—out of control, beyond the reach of reason. His chest was heaving like a bellows as he tried to draw in enough oxygen to think straight. He speared his hands into his hair and hung his head, closing his eyes. Control. He needed control.

Control. She'd lost control—of the situation, of herself. Serena swallowed hard and pressed a hand to her bruised lips. How could this have happened? She didn't even *like* the man. But the instant his mouth had touched hers she had experienced an explosion of desire that had melted everything else. She hadn't thought of anything but his mouth on hers, the taste of him, the strength of his arms, the feel of his body. Shivers rocked through her now like the aftershocks of an earthquake. Heaven help her, she didn't know herself anymore. What had become of her calm self-discipline, her training, her ability to distance herself from a situation and examine it analytically?

You wanted him, Serena. How's that for analysis?

She shook her head a little in stunned disbelief. "I think I would have been safer with the coon hounds," she mumbled.

Something flashed in Lucky's eyes. His expression went cold. "*Non.* You're safe in this house, lady. I'm out of here."

He turned and stormed into the next room. There was a banging of doors that made Serena wince. When he reappeared he was wearing a black T-shirt that hugged his chest like a coat of paint. He shrugged on a shoulder holster. The pistol it cradled looked big enough to bring down an elephant. Serena felt her eyes widen and her jaw drop.

"It's not hunting season." She didn't realize she had spoken aloud, but Lucky turned and gave her a long, very disturbing look, his panther's eyes glowing beneath his heavy dark brows.

"It is for what I'm after," he said in a silky voice.

He pulled the gun and checked the load. The clip slid back into place with a smooth, sinister hiss and click. Then he was gone. He slipped out the door like a shadow, without a sound.

Serena felt the hair rise up on the back of her neck. For a long moment she stood there, frozen with fear in the heat of the night. With an effort she finally forced her feet to move and went to the screen door to look out.

The night was as black as fresh tar with only a sliver of moon shining down on the bayou. The water gleamed like a sheet of glass. She thought she caught a glimpse of Lucky poling his pirogue out toward a stand of cypress, but in a blink he was gone, vanished, as if he were a creature from the darkest side of the night, able to appear and disappear at will.

"Heaven help me," she whispered, brushing her fingertips across her bottom lip. "What have I gotten myself into now?"

MOTHERS
by Gloria Goldreich

MOTHERS is the story of two couples who have happy marriages in common—but very little else. Nina and David Roth live an affluent suburban life. Stacey and Hall Cosgrove, who have been married since high school, face a future of scraping to get by. There's another difference: the Cosgroves have three children; the Roths cannot conceive. One obstetrician knows of the Roth's desperate wish for a child, just as he knows how easily Stacey Cosgrove is able to conceive—and how much her family needs money. A financial agreement is made for Stacey to carry David's child. However, what starts out as a business arrangement cannot remain simple when human lives are involved. A rare bond of shared motherhood forms between the two women, but as the birth nears, an event occurs that breaks all their careful preparations apart. . . .

TOUCHED BY THORNS
by Susan Bowden

For seventeen idyllic years, lovely, strong-willed Katherine Radcliffe, heroine of TOUCHED BY THORNS, had led a charmed existence on her family's estate in Yorkshire. Suddenly, in one night of shattering tragedy, her beloved Radcliffe Manor is lost to her. Betrayed, then imprisoned, she is rescued by the handsome, mysterious Captain Brendan Fitzgerald, a distant cousin and now rightful heir to Radcliffe Manor. Mesmerized by Katherine's uncommon beauty and fiery disposition, he falls deeply in love and strikes a marriage "bargain" to which she, determined to regain Radcliffe at any cost, reluctantly agrees. Slowly, almost against her will, she finds herself succumbing to Brendan's tenderness and the fierce passions she senses lie just beneath the surface of his gallant demeanor.

FANFARE

On Sale in APRIL
THE FIREBIRDS

☐ 29613-2 $4.99/5.99 in Canada
by Beverly Byrne
author of THE MORGAN WOMEN

The third and final book in Beverly Byrne's remarkable trilogy of passion and revenge. The fortunes of the House of Mendoza are stunningly resolved in this contemporary romance.

FORTUNE'S CHILD

☐ 29424-5 $5.50/6.50 in Canada
by Pamela Simpson

Twenty years ago, Christina Fortune disappeared. Now she's come home to claim what's rightfully hers. But is she an heiress . . . or an imposter?

SEASON OF SHADOWS

☐ 29589-6 $5.99/6.99 in Canada
by Mary Mackey

Lucy and Cassandra were polar opposites, but from the first day they met they became the best of friends. Roommates during the turbulent sixties, they stood beside each other through fiery love affairs and heartbreaking loneliness.

☐ Please send me the books I have checked above. I am enclosing $ _____ (add $2.50 to cover postage and handling). Send check or money order, no cash or C. O. D.'s please.

Mr./ Ms. _____

Address _____

City/ State/ Zip _____

Send order to: Bantam Books, Dept. FN, 414 East Golf Road, Des Plaines, IL 60016

Allow four to six weeks for delivery.

Prices and availability subject to change without notice.

THE SYMBOL OF GREAT WOMEN'S FICTION FROM BANTAM

Ask for these books at your local bookstore or use this page to order.

FN39 - 4/92